THE LON

NICK FLETCHER is an award-w_____ _____ who has worked as a crime reporter and a showbiz journalist. His British private eye creation Max Slater is described by one reviewer as 'a new and riveting anti-hero' and another says Slater has 'all the hallmarks of the classic private eye.'.

In this novel, Max Slater - a former journalist turned private eye - is struggling to make sense of a brutal, inexplicable contract killing in a quiet Devonshire village, but uses dogged persistence along with inspiration from his fictional detective idol, Raymond Chandler's Philip Marlowe, to unravel a complex multiple murder case.

This slick fast-paced thriller is set in Britain and America and is flecked throughout with a sharp cynical wit redolent of classic man-against-the-odds detective fiction.

NICK FLETCHER

THE LONG SUNSET

Ⓒℬ
Classic Books

Published by Classic Books
TQ5 0HG

Printed in Great Britain by TJ International Ltd
Padstow, Cornwall

All rights reserved

Copyright Nick Fletcher 2017

The right of Nick Fletcher to be identified as the author
of this work has been asserted in accordance with
Section 77 of the Copyright, Designs and Patents Act 1988.

This book is sold subject to the condition that it shall not, by way of trade or
otherwise, be lent, resold, hired out or otherwise circulated without the
publisher's prior consent in any form of binding or cover other than that in
which it is published and without a similar condition including this condition
being imposed on the subsequent purchaser.

British Library Cataloguing in Publication Data.
A catalogue record for this book is available from the British Library.

ISBN 978-0-9519399-8-7

Editorial Consultant
Eve Kerswill

AUTHOR'S NOTE

In my early years as a journalist, I worked as a crime reporter but that experience was not the catalyst for my wanting to write crime novels. Instead, I owe my inspiration to novelist Raymond Chandler, whose private eye Philip Marlowe left an indelible stamp on crime writing, taking it from low-level pulp fiction to recognition at the heights of American literature.

Marlowe, a loner who mixed idealism and cynicism with a strong sense of justice, appeared initially in short stories, but in 1939 Chandler published his first Marlowe novel, The Big Sleep. Six other novels followed over the next two decades, establishing Philip Marlowe as an iconic and - to many crime writers - inspirational character.

My own detective creation Max Slater is an ex-journalist turned private eye who also admires Philip Marlowe and is driven by the same need to see justice done, even if on occasion he has to step outside the law. Max first appeared in my short-story collection Escaping The Rain. Since then he has featured in six novellas collectively titled Snapshot, and in a full-length novel, Imperfect Day.

This latest novel recounts a case from early in his career, when the callous murder of an elderly woman in the idyllic Devonshire town of Dartmouth sets Max on the trail of a multiple killer.

For assistance with certain aspects of this book, my thanks are due to journalists and valued friends Neil Bonner and Mark Slack for wise counsel, to retired police officer Trevor Cotterill for specialist advice, and to Judy David, a Senior Lecturer in Psychology at Staffordshire University whose impressive expertise in the criminal mind was invaluable.

Nick Fletcher
South Devon, England

Also by Nick Fletcher

Novels
Imperfect Day

Short Story Collections
Escaping The Rain
Snapshot

Poetry
Dark Heart
Lost Avenues

www.nickfletcher.co.uk

1

My viewpoint was directly behind the killer so my sight of the victim was much the same as his. We could both see a thin, paper-skinned old woman who was blind and deaf and strapped into a gleaming chromium-plated wheelchair.

I was already aware he was going to kill her but advance knowledge did nothing to alleviate the jolting shock of the act, which was carried out with such swiftness and complete unconcern that it became sub-human. The execution, for there is no other way to describe it, took 9.2 seconds. I timed it on a stop-watch.

He fired the gun twice, aiming at her forehead from a distance of about four feet. It is hard to think of any advantage in being blind except not being able to see such a death coming. Marjorie's head dropped, her chin digging deep into the ruched lace frill of her blouse. She had two new sightless yet staring eyes, each weeping blood in surprisingly meagre trickles.

The killer had walked into the room with straight-line briskness. It was just four paces from door to victim and the gun was already in his right hand. He was wearing a dark raincoat and a snap-brimmed hat, and as soon as he fired the two shots, he did a crisp heel-and-toe turn and walked out of the room. I clicked the stop-watch as he went out of the door.

The whole event, entrance and exit, life to death took 9.2 seconds.

I saw his face and for a second or two I thought I would always remember it. Then I realised there would be no need. The straggling moustache and the heavy spectacles were so over-stated, so deliberately theatrical, he was actually advertising the disguise. It was a disappointment, but not a surprise. Only a professional could have carried out such a clinical, robotic killing and been so at ease with himself he chose to flaunt his confidence.

I had wanted to intervene. I had to stop myself leaping from my chair. I wanted to scream a warning. I wanted to wrestle the gunman to the floor, halt the progress of such unrelenting evil. But I couldn't. I was the witness who wasn't there.

I was watching it on a CCTV clip, months later, and yet it still had the power and the presence to evoke the same cold rage I would have felt had I been there when it occurred.

The clip of that awful, shocking, sickening incident had been transferred to DVD and the disc had clattered onto my desk two days ago. It bounced once and bumped against my cup with just enough force to splash a little tea over the rim.

I looked up and there was Krista Carlton, tall and elegant, an instant presence in the room, five-feet-ten if you included the high heels, and leaning over my desk in a tailored crimson two-piece suit with flushed cheeks to match. She was making a good effort to appear calm and controlled but I could see an artery pulsating in her neck.

'Look at it,' she said, pointing at the disc. 'Just look at it.'
There had been no hello, no handshake, no inquiries about my state of health. Straight in the door, straight to the point. She was my two o'clock appointment and she was precisely on time.

I looked her over once again, not just to seek the tiny telling clues that detectives are supposed to notice, but because I liked looking at pretty women. She had long straight dark hair and dark-brown eyes. I rated her as confident, assured, and probably used to getting her own way. Today though, she was edgy, even angry, and she needed help. Why else would she be in the office of the least-known detective in the directory?

Krista had telephoned to make an appointment at nine that

morning, demanding to see me as soon after immediately as possible. I could have seen her at ten, but I pushed her back to 2pm to give the impression I was busy. It's best not to appear too eager, even when this might turn out to be only my fifth case this year. And we're in September.

When I had asked her the nature of her problem, she said that if she told me on the telephone, I wouldn't take the case. She wanted to make an appointment so she could at least yell at my face when I said no. She had achieved her objective. She had my attention.

The DVD lay between us, the focal point of tension. 'Look at it,' she repeated, a flash of impatience showing through. 'What are you waiting for? Your fee?'

She reached for her clutch-bag, slim and neat and black and looking so expensive it didn't need to show a designer badge.

'No,' I told her. 'I'm waiting for the context. Whatever's on the disc will mean a lot more if I know why it's made you so upset.'

'You think this is upset? I'm mad as hell.'

'I know. I was just being polite.'

She sat on the leather armchair in front of my desk. Someone had taught her how to sit. She was perched on the edge, upright, with knees together.

'Coffee?'

'What kind?'

'The kind that comes in a jar. I don't have Columbian, decaf, mocca, chocca or wocca. If I could afford that kind of coffee, I'd have an office in a better part of town.'

'Just black,' she said. 'Is there really a wocca?'

I gave her the wry smile that always looked good in my bathroom mirror, but never seemed to work that well anywhere else.

My office was a twelve by fifteen box on the ground floor of a tall Victorian terrace on the southern edge of Exeter, a gentile town not greatly in need of private detectives, nor motorists it seemed as it was so difficult to drive into the town centre, and which might help explain why I got so few cases. But I liked the West Country. Though born and raised in Shropshire, as a kid I'd often holidayed in Devon with my parents.

After I quit journalism to become a private detective, I'd set up office in Shrewsbury but then my parents retired to Devon, and before long I followed. I liked the mild climate, the palm trees, the clear night skies and the beguiling belief among the locals that there was absolutely nothing in life that ever needed doing quickly.

Of course, the low crime rate in Devon indicated it was less than fertile territory in which to set up as a new Philip Marlowe - my detective hero created in the 1930s by Raymond Chandler - but I had enough money to tide me over for a year or two, so that didn't matter too much. I could be selective, and learn the trade gradually.

I'd furnished the office with old oak furniture which came cheaply from a local auction room. I could afford newer and better but I wanted the worn and slightly faded look favoured by Marlowe. 'Reasonably shabby' was how he described his office.

Krista was looking around too, while I poured hot water on the instant granules.

The door into my office was directly opposite my desk, a big, wide battleship of a desk that had plenty of room for my collection of things you put on your desk to create an impression. There was the Art Deco black marble inkstand in the form of a Sphinx, my replica Bakelite telephone, my chromium-plated desk lamp in the shape of a DC9 aeroplane, and two square-framed photographs. One was a sepia portrait of Madeleine Carroll - the most beautiful actress in pre-war movies - and the other showed a German Shepherd dog sitting proud as only a dog can. The day I moved into the office, I spent an hour just arranging the items on the desk. Yet Krista didn't seem to notice my efforts. She chose to stare out of the window.

The bottom line of my advertisement read: POSITIVELY NO ROUTINE CASES HANDLED

It cut out the time-wasters and the grind of serving writs and tracking errant husbands. It also explained why I was severely under-employed.

'Good advertising always works,' I said.

'It just means you're good at advertising. It doesn't necessarily follow that you're a good detective,' she said sharply. 'That's why I had you checked out.'

Checked out? How?' I was a little insulted and my tone showed it.

She used the smile she'd probably been using since she was 14 to bring men to heel. 'I couldn't ask you to help me without knowing if you were up to the job, could I?'

'So I come recommended?'

'Quite the opposite. I was told you were untrained and inexperienced and that I would be a fool to use you.'

'Who told you that?'

'The other private detective.'

'What other private detective?'

'The one I hired to check out whether it was worth hiring you.'

'Maybe I just misheard you,' I said. 'I thought for a moment you said you had hired someone to tell you if I was good enough to hire.'

'That's what I said.'

'Then why didn't you hire him?'

'Oh, he was completely wrong for the job,' she said dismissively. 'He was the sort of man who wore brown shoes with a blue suit. Worse than that, he was an ex-policeman.'

'Perhaps you would have been better off with an ex-policeman. At least he would be trained and experienced.'

'I can see I've upset you,' she said, leaning forward in the chair.

'This is upset? I'm mad as hell.'

She smiled at my quoting back her own words, and it eased the slight souring of the moment. 'Look, I know you might feel slighted but I had to do it. This thing is too important to entrust to the wrong man.'

I sat back, sipping my coffee. So far, I had concluded Krista Carlton was rich, well-educated, very confident and exactly the sort of person you don't expect to be seeking help from a one-man detective agency at the cheap end of town. Time to find out just what this was all about. But first, my ruffled vanity needed to be unruffled.

'Just who did you get to check me out?'

'His name was McKelvey. Do you know him?'

I knew McKelvey. He was an ex-CID sergeant who took early retirement at 50 and was now boosting his police pension with routine leg-work for the courts or insurance companies. He was no Columbo but he was thorough and reliable. And he was right about me on all counts.

'What did he tell you?' I just had to know.

'You really want the details?'

'Why not?'

She clicked open her bag and pulled out a tiny notepad with a silver cover.

'Slater, Max. Aged 40. Ex-journalist. Quit the Star two years ago after receiving a one-tenth share of a £4 million office syndicate lottery win. Set up as a private detective. Lifelong ambition, according to interview he gave to a local newspaper at the time. Said he always wanted to be like Raymond Chandler's private eye Philip Marlowe.'

She looked up. 'There's more. Shall I read Mr McKelvey's conclusion?'

'Why spare me now?'

Her eyes dipped down to the notebook again. 'Slater is untrained and inexperienced,' she read, voice as stern as a teacher delivering a bad school report. 'In my professional opinion, it would be a serious error to even consider hiring him for any task more complex than finding a lost dog.'

Krista closed the notebook. 'That's it,' she said. 'You did ask. Anyway, I'm sure he was exaggerating.'

I sat upright. I leaned forward, elbows on the edge of my desk, hands clasped in front of me. Maybe it was too much to look professional, or even competent. I decided the best bet was honesty.

'I wouldn't necessarily choose those particular phrases myself,' I said, trying to sound not the least defensive. 'And I could of course point out that McKelvey might be just a touch biased, maybe angling for the case himself. But on the whole, what he says is true.'

I paused for a couple of seconds to see if she was surprised by the admission, but she said nothing. She just looked at me with an expression even a man who is good at first impressions couldn't fathom.

'So why are you here?' I asked, clipping my tone to standard business mode. 'Why do you want me when you could have any amount of experienced, dependable detectives?'

'The reason I want you, Mr Slater, is quite simple. It's because you have so much to prove.'

That was one reason I hadn't considered.

'I don't mean prove to other people,' she added helpfully. 'I mean prove to yourself. I want someone who will be determined and persistent. Someone who, unlike ex-policemen, won't be afraid to bend the rules. Or break them. Forgive my mentioning this again, but from what I gather, in your profession, you're perceived as a no-hoper. For the right man, that can be quite an incentive. Question is, are you the right man?'

The DVD that had bought Krista Carlton into my office lay there like a slim flat ticking bomb waiting to explode its shocking contents. I picked it up and slid it into the player behind my desk.

'Let's find out,' I said, though I already knew the answer.

There were a couple of minutes of near-silence after the disc ended. I say near-silence because I could hear myself breathing harshly, as if I had run up a flight of stairs. I hadn't known what to expect when I put in the disc, but it wasn't that. I went to pick up my coffee cup. I didn't want the coffee, it was long cold anyway. I just wanted something to do. I couldn't grip the handle tight enough to lift the cup. Fingers wouldn't work. After two minutes, the sickening shock of seeing a crippled old lady shot dead in her wheelchair eased as anger warmed my blood and stimulated the senses.

'Who was she?' I looked across at Krista. She was still and white and her eyes were ice-chunks with mascara borders.

'My Aunt Marjorie. She was 85. She lived in Dartmouth, in Devon. She was blind and deaf and couldn't walk. She could not possibly have had an enemy in the world.'

It suddenly clicked into context. I remembered the case now. It had been headline news about a year ago, generating pages of mammoth black tabloid headlines. MOST CALLOUS MURDER IN HISTORY and variations on that theme.

Biggest police hunt in years. Months on, no progress, no suspect, no leads. Last I heard a team of 20 cops were still working on it. Despite TV appeals, a £100,000 reward on offer, and the bludgeoning pressure of the media demanding a culprit, there was not even a faint lead to follow. Even after being caught on security tape, the killer hadn't been seen before the event, or after it. No witnesses, no obvious motive.

'I'm sorry,' I said. 'I found it tough to watch, let alone you.'

'I've watched it 17 times,' she said. 'I get upset every time I see it. Even carrying it into your office upset me. I've made myself watch it time after time. I always think I'll see something that wasn't there before. Something that will explain why.'

Why was the big question. That was the question on every newspaper front-page, on every TV talk show and on the lips of every bar-room pundit for weeks after the murder.

Krista shifted position, transferring her weight from left elbow to right hip. 'The police won't publicly say they've given up,' she said. 'Privately, they more or less admit it. They say they have to scale down, there are other cases, lack of resources, the file will remain open. Usual shit.'

'I'm flattered you think I might succeed where the entire UK police force has failed, but McKelvey was right. I'm not your man.'

She made direct eye contact and said coolly: 'Positively no routine cases handled?'

Maybe not coolly. Maybe the question was frosted with disdain.

'I didn't say I wouldn't take the case. I just said I wasn't your man. Big difference.'

She looked quizzical. At least that's how I interpreted the raised eyebrow.

'I'm not good enough for this kind of case. I've no experience. I was never in the police force. And however much money you might offer me, it will never buy the kind of resources the police have already thrown at it. If you want a private detective, there are better ones. Almost any of them in the phone book will be better. However, if you choose to ignore all that good advice, then yes, I'll take the case.'

Her face was impassive but I could guess what was coming. I could read people.

'I knew you would,' she said.

'I knew you'd know I would.'

We might have smiled except for the memory of Marjorie, asleep forever in that shiny chariot .

People are like radios. You meet them, and within a few sentences, you are trying to get their wavelength. Some, you just find on the fringe, the absolute extremities of your frequency. Conversation is hard going. You can just about relate to them if you work at it. But others, you just tune into quickly, and they to you. That's how I felt it was now. After some initial tuning, we were on the same frequency, the same station.

'I suppose you'll want to know why there's a recording of the murder,' she said.

There you are. I was just going to ask. Radio waves.

She explained that Marjorie Wilkes may have been blind, deaf and immobile but she was fiercely independent. She insisted on living in her own home, leading her own life in her own small, limited way. She didn't want anyone - family or otherwise - living in, but permitted paid helpers from the village who called several times a day to check on her, prepare meals, run errands. And there were the security cameras.

'My brother Guy had them installed,' said Krista. 'He lives about ten miles away and he had a monitoring system put in so he could keep an eye on her. She never knew about it, of course. She would have never have allowed it. But it gave us peace of mind. It came in useful once, when she somehow managed to slip out of her wheelchair and couldn't climb back. Guy would check the monitors several times a day. He noticed the situation and rang one of her helpers and they went around. Of course, they said they called by chance. They were paid well enough to keep quiet about the cameras, at least to her.'

'Would many other people know about them, outside of neighbours and the family?'

'Hard to say. Not many, I suppose.'

'The killer did. He looked up at the camera as he left. It seemed to me it was a deliberate act.'

'I thought so too. He just didn't care. He may as well have stuck up two fingers.'

'He did, in his own way,' I said. 'And that's what so odd. Professional killers aren't usually arrogant, or if they are, they don't flaunt it. They're meticulously careful, because their careers depend on it. So when a hitman spots a security camera, he either takes the disc or hard-drive if he has time, or if he knew in advance, he would use a disguise. The odd thing here is that it seems he actually wanted to leave the video evidence. He wanted the murder to be seen, to be re-played. He was making a point.'

She nodded. 'But why would he do that?'

'What have the police told you? What's their theory?'

'There have been several family meetings with senior detectives, the most recent was last week,' she said. 'They're certain it was a contract killing, as they put it, yet despite all the time they've put in, they have no idea why Marjorie was killed. That's what prompted me to contact you. I'm sure the police have done their best, but it makes me so angry that whoever did it has got away with it.'

The wide eyes, flushed face and pursed lips gave her the spark her cool distant persona needed.

'In the movies, people are killed because they witnessed something,' she said.'But Marjorie couldn't have seen anything, or overheard anything. She hadn't even left the house for at least five years.'

This did seem a motive you could discard. The blind and deaf inhabit a world where you don't witness anything except your own ghosts. 'What about mistaken identity?'I suggested. 'Maybe the hitman had the wrong target.'

Krista looked to the ceiling in exasperation. 'You mean there's another blind and deaf old lady out there who has upset someone enough to have her killed? I don't think so!'

'What I meant was that the hitman may have been given the wrong address, or no description of the victim, or...or you're right. I'm talking rubbish. This murder has every hallmark of a highly professional hit, and I'm trying to suggest he might have made a mistake! I told you to get someone else.'

I tried the old ruse of speaking louder and more positively. It sometimes restores a little credibility. 'The killer would have been properly briefed,' I added unnecessarily. 'When they're that good, neither they nor whoever hires them makes that kind of mistake.'

So it was two theories down, and time to put up another. I didn't want to ask my next question, but it had to be asked, and I was sure the police had asked it anyway. Even so, I braced myself for a possible explosion. 'There's another reason people are often killed,' I told her, as flat and matter-of-fact I as I could be. 'So tell me - who inherits?'

Krista took the question without even momentary hesitation, and with no visible resentment.

'I do.'

'Just you?'

'Just me. I was always Aunt Marjorie's favourite. She made no secret of that.'

'Did your brother know?'

'Guy knew, and so did my sister Olivia. When Aunt Marjorie made her will a few years ago, she called us all together and announced what she was going to do. Nobody minded.'

'It might just have appeared that way.'

'I don't think so. We're all close, and in any case, Guy and Olivia are already set for life. Daddy left them two million each when he died, plus income from property and shares. Marjorie was comfortably off, but what she left they probably wouldn't even notice in their bank accounts.'

'That leaves you then.' I knew she wouldn't mind the inference. She'd know this had to be cleared up before I could move on.

'Daddy left me much the same,' she told me, almost apologetically. 'It was sweet of Auntie but I told her at the time I didn't need the money and that she should leave it all to a dogs' home.'

'Let's re-cap, 'I said, trying to buy time to find some fresh ideas. 'So far, it seems very doubtful Marjorie was killed to silence her, or for her money. So let's explore another possibility. Hitman are often hired to administer retribution. Could be revenge, someone wanting to get even, maybe settle a grudge from the past. Even sweet old ladies can have their secrets.'

We both sat silent. The problem with this theory was that you couldn't rule it out unless you knew the secret.

'A killer this clinical was top-drawer,' I said. 'He would be known only to a select few who paid large enough fees for him to need to work very little. Maybe just two or three times a year. Such a man would be very hard to find unless you were in on that very exclusive circle, or at least knew someone who was. Just ask yourself - if you wanted a class-act hitman, where would you start looking?'

She shrugged.

'Exactly,' I said. 'Even if you've seen enough crime movies and have enough money, it isn't easy if you don't have the connections. There isn't a Hitman heading in the Yellow Pages, you can't do an internet search, and you can't start asking in a bar. All you'll end up with is a visit from the police. The professional hitman operates on another level, a world of guarded contacts, trusted recommendations, meetings through mutual friends. More executions are arranged on the golf course than they are in seedy bars.'

'Was that newspaper feature right about you being caught up with the movie image of the private eye?' Krista leaned back in the armchair and uncrossed her legs.

'Partly. I loved Bogart playing Philip Marlowe. Always

wanted to be Bogart, but younger. He was nearly 50 when he made The Big Sleep. Too old for the part.'

'Not to old to attract Lauren Bacall. And not just in the film, she became his wife.'

I was surprised she knew that. 'He had a lot of charisma,' I said. 'Maybe that did the trick.'

She didn't reply and I didn't know where to take the conversation. The silence suddenly felt awkward so I got up and went to switch on the kettle. I made some more coffee and looked out across the street. The morning had been warm and bright, but now vast, puffed-up black clouds daubed the skyline and a misty rain had drifted in. It made the day somehow feel sour and disagreeable. I turned and noticed how dark the office had become. Half-shadowed as she sat sipping her coffee, Krista was still neatly perched on the edge of the chair. I stayed by the window.

'What's the next step?' she asked. 'What do you plan to do now?'

Until then, I hadn't thought what to do, so I made an obvious suggestion. 'I'd like to go through Majorie's personal effects, her paperwork mainly. The police won't have missed anything, but it might help give me a better picture of her life.'

'All her papers are in three boxes in the boot of my car,' said Krista, handing me the keys. 'I thought that's where a detective would start.'
She didn't offer to help me fetch the boxes, so I went out to her silver BMW Z4 sports car parked across the street and carried them back myself. They were dark-green boxes, office-style, with stiff card lids.

'I'd also like to visit Marjorie's house, if that's possible,' I told her. 'I don't know why, because so long after the event I'm not going to find a vital clue, even if I had the powers of Sherlock Holmes. I just feel it's the place to begin.'

Krista nodded. 'That's not a problem. I live there now. It's in Dartmouth.'

'What about tomorrow?'

'I can be available. What time?'

We agreed to meet at 11am and I jotted down the address. She hadn't asked about my fees and I didn't feel I should mention money at that stage. We said a business-like goodbye, and I gave some suitable clichéd reassurances.

I saw her to the door, and watched her cross the street and get into the BMW. I closed the door, returned to the office and hauled the boxes out through the rear entrance and into the boot of my car. When you live alone, taking that kind of work home with you is a real joy.

Back in the office, I poured more coffee. Across the street, Krista's car hadn't moved off, still waiting for a break in the traffic. The flashing offside indicator spilled pools of amber across the shiny wet surface. It had started to rain hard.

I suppose it was about 10 minutes or so before I happened to glance out of the window again, and her car was still there, indicator still pulsating. Maybe the car wouldn't start and she was too embarrassed to come back and seek help. Maybe she was taking a call on her mobile.

I decided to go outside and check. The car was low and I had to stoop to look inside. Krista seemed surprised to see me. She stared at me, a full eye-contact stare. She was entitled to look surprised. I could see right away she was dead.

Her hair was matted with blood and a thick trickle down the side of her neck was beginning to congeal and form a very passable map of South America. I stood upright, half my mind stunned, half of it racing, wondering how this could have happened. Then I saw how. The Z4 was a convertible. The hood was up but I was looking down on three neat holes in the black fabric, directly above Krista's head. Three bullets, close-range, silenced gun. It was unquestionably a professional hit.

I stayed with the car and used my mobile to call the police. The rain was bouncing off the metalwork like buckshot. My shirt was a second skin but I didn't feel wet, just cold. Down the glass of the driver's door, hundreds of spidering rivulets couldn't mask that white face and startled eyes.

The police were there in five minutes. The blurred blue-light convoy came in fast on the wrong side of the road, and formed a cordon around the Z4 and me. Five of them, all in wetly glinting yellow jackets surrounded me. I was still staring fixedly down at the blanched face of Krista Carlton. They needn't have worried about me leaving the crime-scene. It took two of them to prise me off the car.

2

I was expecting the interview room at the police station to be bleak and dispiriting, a room with grimy grey paintwork, sparse furniture, a solitary light-bulb and, almost certainly, rubber floor tiles so that it would be easy for the cleaner to mop up the blood, sweat and tears that must be splashed around such a place on a daily basis. But it wasn't like that at all. It was pleasant pastel-green, brightly-lit from recessed rectangles of neon tubes. There were several office-style armchairs with dark padded seats, and tables in a strange bleached wood that suggested a large police incident-van had been diverted to IKEA.

I had been requested to give a statement about why Krista had been to see me, and I'd been waiting almost an hour, but that didn't matter. Years of work as a journalist had taught me that the police always keep you waiting. Sometimes it's deliberate, they try to see whether you get worried or stressed or panicky. Sometimes they just don't have enough information to hand to adequately question you. Sometimes the officer assigned to the interview is busy on another case. So I waited. Over by the door, a lone police woman kept me company. She didn't look as though she wanted to chat but each time I glanced at her, she gave me a rather uncertain smile. I spent most of the time thinking what I was going to tell them when they did start questioning me. I decided it would be a good policy to tell them everything, on the grounds that in fact, I knew nothing. I'd just tell it how it happened, and then see what they could tell me.

The silver hands on the dark-blue face of my watch seemed to have been moving at near-terminal slowness. Then there was a heavy footfall in the corridor, the door opened, and in strode a man of quite extraordinary physical appearance. He was tall, around six-feet-six I'd guess, and he was broad too, but muscular not fat. Yet it wasn't really his size that caught the attention. It was his head. It appeared to be square. The sides of his face seemed absolutely vertical and his slim and rather delicate ears were so close to the side of his head that at first you didn't see them at all. His hair, fair but greying slightly and crew-cut in the style favoured by the American forces was also flat-topped. He was pale-skinned, cold-eyed and almost lipless, his mouth just a thin red gash. When he spoke his voice was quite normal and surprisingly friendly. He said he was Inspector Kelp, and cursorily introduced a fat, bearded companion as Sergeant Pearce.

Kelp sat opposite me across the table, opening a folder he had bought into the room with him, apparently glancing over notes. He looked up. 'Now Mr Slater, let's see if you can shed some light on today's events and get you on your way home.' He glanced down at the folder. 'I understand you're a former journalist, so you probably know a little about police procedure. So you'll know you are not under arrest. You're a witness, here to help us with our enquiries. I'm sure you have written that phrase a time or two.'

The corners of his mouth twitched upwards in a small amused smile. 'I further understand, Mr Slater, that you are now a private investigator. Been doing that long, have you?'

I shook my head. 'Couple of years, minor stuff.'

Kelp didn't look too surprised and I was sure he already had that kind of information in his file. I'd given all my basic details including my occupation to a uniformed officer at the crime scene.

'I think I should make something very clear before we move on, Mr Slater,' he said, and I wished he wouldn't keep putting my name into every sentence. I knew who I was. 'As I'm sure you are aware, being a private investigator has no official status in the UK, unlike in America, where they operate a sort of licensing system. Even so, the police there don't much like a private eyes, they feel they can get in the way of solving a crime. I have no view on the matter.'

His eyes said differently.

He asked me to run through the sequence of events since the very moment Krista Carlton had contacted me. As I related it, he was glancing at the folder again, presumably checking if I deviated from the brief account I had given to the uniformed guys. He let me tell it without interruption, but when I finished, he asked me to tell it again. This time he interrupted from time to time, clarifying a point here and there. When I mentioned that Krista had asked me to look into the murder of her aunt, his eyes had narrowed but he didn't comment beyond saying he recalled the case.

'There must be a connection between the two murders,' I ventured. 'It's too much of a co-incidence.'

Kelp's expression was unchanged. 'That possibility will form part of our investigation,' he said.' I would prefer that you didn't continue your own investigation into this matter, though I cannot stop you. Amateurs can both distract and impede a police investigation, so I trust you will leave this one to us. Do we understand each other?'

I nodded agreement, though I was agreeing only that we understood each other.

'Good. I think that will do for now. Sergeant Pearce will take down a formal statement and arrange for someone to take you home.'

There were several questions I wanted to ask but I didn't bother because I knew I'd get no answers. The statement took another half hour and then a patrol car gave me a lift to the office. I didn't want to go home. There was too much on my mind.

It was now mid-evening and getting dark. When I walked into the office, I didn't bother with the main lights, just switched on my desk lamp which cast a mellow glow across the chair where just a few hours earlier, Krista Carlton had been perched with model elegance. I recalled her saying I had a lot to prove, and she was right. The remark stung and so did Kelp dismissing me as an amateur. He was right too. But pride beat logic. Cold logic said I should walk away from the case. My client was dead, and I hadn't even a vague idea of what was going on, let alone where to begin. But my pride said otherwise. I owed it to Krista to do all I could to find her killer, and that of Aunt Marjorie.

I had to start thinking. I took a five-day-old 'emergency' sandwich from the office fridge, made some coffee and laced it with two generous shots of vodka. I sat at my desk, eating, sipping vodka coffee which tasted weird, and pondering the events of a dour and tragic day.

I hadn't seen the actual shooting, but I knew they'd found a couple of witnesses who had seen a motorcyclist pause briefly alongside the BMW because I was still at the scene when a keen young uniformed cop found them. It wasn't hard – they were still standing across the street with their little terrier dog. Husband and wife, in their sixties I'd say. I heard them telling one of the officers that they thought the motorcyclist had just stopped at the car to ask directions. In fact he was just putting three silent shots through the hood fabric. They were able to describe him too. He was wearing black leather, black crash helmet, and had a black motorcycle. That was all they saw from thirty metres away. It was a dead-end description.

A need to get something done, start something off was surging through me. Feelings of increasing inadequacy were setting in. I leaned back in my wood and leather swivel armchair and engaged in what my hero Philip Marlowe always called 'a spot of foot dangling.'

Then I remembered it was usually the telephone that got Marlowe up and about and motivated. Mine didn't ring on cue, despite my hard stare at it, so I decided the next best thing was to make some calls myself. The only people I could think of ringing were Krista's family. I had taken notes during our meeting, so I had their details. I rang her brother Guy, who wasn't pleased about such a late call.

I apologised, and if my condolences sounded mumbled and hurried, it was because I just wanted to get them out of the way. I gave a short account of my meeting with Krista and said that I had arranged with her to look around Marjorie's house, and could I still do that?

Guy wasn't a happy man. Okay, no one who had just had a sister murdered was going to be happy. I meant he wasn't happy with me investigating. I also got the impression he thought that if Krista hadn't come to see me, she would still be alive. Wrong impression, of course. Krista had been followed. If the gunman hadn't killed her outside my office, it would have been somewhere else. He just took the opportunity when it presented itself. I didn't bother explaining that to Guy, I just pressed him to let me visit, lied that I had made a promise to his dead sister, and the lie clinched it for me. We arranged to meet the next day at the house in Dartmouth that had once been Marjorie's and latterly Krista's .

I didn't quite know what to make of Guy, but then I didn't quite know what to make of anything that had happened so far. I sat there reviewing the day, aided by few more shots of vodka, this time without the coffee. My thoughts circled, time passed, nothing happened. I was still at the start. Eventually, I glanced at my watch, surprised to see it was well after 2am. Too much vodka ruled out driving home and I was about to unfold a camp-bed I kept in the cupboard when I heard a sharp cracking sound from the direction of the back door at the end of the short corridor leading from the rear car-park to my office. The splintering crack was the door being forced. Then I heard footsteps.

Tackling burglars is bold and brave, especially as these days many of them carry knives or even guns. But it was also stupid. In the few seconds I had, I did the only thing I could think of. My big oak desk was the kneehole type, two pedestals, flat top and small cave where your knees fit. I crawled into the cave and squashed myself in as far as I could get, like a hibernating bear.

The bulb in the desk lamp was only 40 watts. It put light on the desk but little elsewhere, so my cave was just a big black hole. I heard the office door open and a pause while the intruder scanned the room. My interpretation of the sound pattern over the next 10 minutes wasn't all that clever. Anyone could have worked out from what they could hear that a search was taking place. Now and then I glimpsed a flashlight arc across the carpet or along the wall. Whoever it was began with the filing cabinets, then moved over to my desk. I'd concluded early on this wasn't likely to be a random burglary. Houses provide more valuables than an office. And the search was detailed, as if something specific was being sought. My guess was that this was somehow connected to Krista.

Now the top of the desk was being examined, which wouldn't take long. There was my diary, which would reveal my appointment with Krista, and then I realised that my notes from my interview with her were readily visible too. I'd been re-reading them. There was a long pause while I imagined they were being read. Luckily, it was all just factual stuff, and in any case my hand-writing is almost illegible, partly shorthand from my journalistic days. My notes would disclose nothing significant, apart from the one thing that was very significant. The notes left no doubt that I was working on the Krista Carlton case.

There were seven drawers in my desk, three in each side-pedestal, and a wider one across the centre. None of them was locked. The intruder checked each, though I knew they contained nothing of any use, unless it was helpful to know I read Devon Life magazine and used a battery shaver. He worked both sides of the desk, but he didn't see me. I had made myself so thin, I was virtually papered to the woodwork. Then he came to the middle drawer and sat in my chair. Fortunately, he had to pull the chair back to make room to pull open the drawer so his knees were just short of my shaking shoulder. I was so scared to turn my head, I was trying to see out of my left ear. As he shoved paperwork back into the drawer, something fell. It was a single sheet of paper, a note, maybe a receipt. I didn't much care what it was, just where it landed. I watched with entranced horror as it floated lazily down, a stark silhouette against the yellow back-light of the desk lamp. It drifted into my cave.

3

It was one of those bleak grey mornings with a knife-edged wind and sudden bursts of cold, penetrating rain, yet I was delighted to see it. It meant I was still alive.

Kelp had summoned a crime-scene team to my office at 3am, just 20 minutes after my phone call. His flinty eyes were judgemental and his tone was as terse as it could get without straying into a stronger adjective. He told me an adventurous ten year old could have broken in to my office and asked why didn't I have deadlocks and an alarm system. He reminded me that it was purely luck that I hadn't been found hiding under my desk, and probably killed.

He was right, of course. When that paper had fluttered down, nose-diving towards me, I expected to be staring into someone's face. I heard my chair creak as the intruder leaned forward, but only a long arm reached down. A big surgical-gloved hand plucked up the sheet of paper and the drawer closed. As he stood up, his legs from the knees down were briefly in view, faintly lit by the down-arc of the desk lamp. All I could see were black trousers and black slip-on shoes with a small brass decorative motif on the side. It was in the form of a rodeo rider.

I heard his footsteps fade from the room and from the building but I stayed in the deep, safe womb of my cave for another five minutes before I crept out on my hands and knees, fearful as a baby rabbit leaving its burrow for the first time, and called the police. When I mentioned Kelp's name and said he should be informed immediately, the duty officer really got things moving.

Now the crime scene guys were packing up their equipment and Kelp said he was heading for the police canteen for an

27

early breakfast. To his credit, he waited for everyone to leave the room before he gave me a brutally-phrased lecture. I'd like to say I couldn't remember exactly what he said, but I can. You don't forget invective of that magnitude. Certainly the phrase 'bungling amateur' still resonated.

Kelp told me stay away from the case, make no more enquiries and preferably go stay with friends for a few days until he had a clearer picture of just what was going on. But to do that only after giving him the some contact numbers. I agreed to everything, but his narrow-eyed stare suggested he knew I was saying merely what I thought he wanted to hear. I think he knew that my intentions were completely different.

Next day was bright and fresh and full of promise. My meeting with Guy Carlton was at 2pm and the cottage in Dartmouth was a 90-minute drive, due south from through pleasant countryside. Before setting out, I spent time making a detailed appraisal of the clutter of papers that served as a sad memorial to Marjorie's life. Thankfully I hadn't unloaded them from the boot of my car. The papers didn't need expert appraisal. A bright chimpanzee could have quickly gathered that here was a life of utter normality, trenched in routine village and family activities. There was a lot of stuff like old photographs from years before the old dear lost her sight, showing her to be quite a looker in a permed-hair, long-skirted sort of way. There were bank statements, insurance policies, old birthday cards, out-dated brochures. There were letters from solicitors relating to the sale of a painting, auction receipts for the disposal of furniture, a folder containing a wad of share certificates, a copy of her will, and various letters from charities asking for donations, or thanking her for making them. There was a bundle of letters from a friend called Enid, dating from the 1940s and petering out in the 1960s. There was even the handbook for a 1949 Armstrong Siddeley car. It's surprising what people keep, especially someone who had been blind for years. Not one single item caused even a remote ripple of suspicion, nor generated even a tiny need for further enquiry. My disappointment was intense.

I set off far too early for my appointment with Guy Carlton.

I didn't want to be late, and also didn't want to be stuck in the office pondering the case. A sleepless night churning the sparse facts hadn't provided any fresh angles, the examination of Marjorie's papers had yielded nothing.

The journey from Exeter to Dartmouth was unusually smooth, free from roadworks which seemed almost permanent in the West Country. I was still far too early for my appointment and I needed a break from the mental chess of moving the paucity of facts around an endless loop so on a whim I diverted to the fishing port of Brixham, which I hadn't visited for several years and where I had holidayed as a child. Very little seemed to have changed. Cottages clustered around the pretty harbour, jammed tightly into the steep hillside, peering over one another like curious onlookers.

The harbour was dominated by a full-size replica of the Golden Hind, the ship used by Francis Drake to sail around the world. He wasn't born in Brixham, and hadn't set off from there on his epic voyage, but Drake was at the centre of the Spanish Armada battles which were strung out along the English channel and thus past Torbay so there was that historical association with the legendary hero. The Golden Hind in Brixham harbour tapped into this connection and was a good tourist attraction, part of the charm and appeal of a town which also had a colourful smuggling history.

It was a still, sunlit day, the boats barely moving on their mooring, the sea too lazy to make an effort. I walked along the quayside for a few minutes, watching holidaymakers enjoying fish and chips or cream teas at pavement cafes. I envied their carefree relaxation, their enjoyment of a beautiful day, the total normality of their lives. The envy lasted only for seconds. My life couldn't be quiet and normal because I could never get that death-face image of Marjorie out of my mind. At least until I found who killed her. The realisation jolted me, a sharp reminder that I had grim business ahead.

I walked slowly back to my car and drove up the narrow winding hill towards Kingswear, where I was catching the small car-ferry across the estuary to Dartmouth. I had to wait a few minutes for the ferry, which took just eight cars at a time across the 200 metre span of calm water. As we moved off, I sat entranced by the sight of four tiers of houses packed tight along the hillside opposite, all in random colours like the painting of an adventurous child.

The ferryman grounded the ramp and I drove off, sweeping right down a narrow street and then sharp left to wind up the hill towards the cottage where Marjorie had been murdered. The houses and cottages were tightly packed and well-maintained, many probably holiday homes in a town that bordered on being almost too pretty for its own good. Having too many part-time residents risked it losing its community heart but for now, it appeared the town council might have the balance about right. Looping the car left, I followed the road down Crowther's Hill towards where Marjorie had lived. Properties began to look more expensive, with neat gardens and shrub-edged driveways. When I was given directions, I'd been told to look out for Guy's silver Audi estate car as a marker – it would be in front of Marjorie's cottage. I spotted the Audi almost immediately and turned into the gravel drive which curved around a neatly trimmed lawn with a central flower bed of contrasting sea grasses and straggling lavender. The cottage was set back, its weathered grey stone flecked with ivy. The front door was painted dark matt blue and there was a large brass knocker in the form of an open-mouthed fish. I rapped it twice.

The man who opened the door was in his early forties, with dark floppy hair which was a month late for a cut. Ten years ago he would have been considered handsome, now he was just carrying a little fat, cheeks drooping, and the start of a double chin evident. He wore a dark-grey suit, pale blue shirt and claret-coloured tie with an overlarge knot. 'I take it you're Slater,' he said as if I was already an irritant. 'You'd best come in.'

Guy Carlton was a tedious and monotonous man, and so was our conversation. Yes, he was shocked, no, he'd no idea Krista was coming to see me. Yes, the family was baffled, and no, they definitely did not want a private detective looking into the matter. The police were professionals doing all they could. And what was it I wanted anyway?

Just then there was the sound of another car outside, and through the small-paned window I saw a woman who looked like Krista Carlton getting out of red Porsche Boxster. She walked in and introduced herself as Olivia, Krista's sister. They weren't twins, but they looked it. She was almost as tall, and her hair was almost as long, but she somehow lacked the immediate presence of Krista, the self-assurance. Olivia had a softer mouth and less sparky eyes, though it was early to make a full judgement. She wore a crisp light grey trouser suit which looked expensively cut, and matt black leather shoes with a square toe and low chunky heel.

'Good afternoon, Mr Slater,' she said. Her voice was firm but subdued, yet she did smile, and added 'Thank you for coming.'

Given that I'd forced myself on them, I thought that was nice of her. Guy had evidently briefed her on the reason I was there. She offered me coffee and asked if there was anything specific I wanted to look at.

'To be honest, I don't know,' I said. 'I'd like to be able to tell you I have some idea of what this is all about, but I have no idea at all. If I may, I'd like to start by looking through Krista's things.'

Guy, who had been over by the window putting his scowl through its full repertoire, was shaking his head in silent objection, but Olivia ignored him. 'Start in the study,' she said, pointing to a door on the right. Guy strode out of the room, angry but not protesting. Maybe I had misjudged Olivia.

She showed me into a small square room with magnolia paintwork and low exposed beams. It was deftly sprinkled with delicate Victorian furniture, prints and ornaments, rather like a film-set antiques shop. I made my way over to a petite mahogany writing desk with a deep burgundy leather top, and opened a drawer.

'Did the police go through all this stuff yesterday?' I asked Olivia, who had brought in a cup of coffee.

'They were here for hours. I think they went through everything,' she said. 'Of course, they sifted everything of Marjorie's at the time she was murdered too. There was nothing of any significance.'

'And what about Krista's things?'

'They took away her diary, various papers, and her laptop. They asked me a lot about her, lifestyle, relationships, that sort of thing.'

'Boyfriend?'

'No one right now. I gave them details of previous ones I knew of, but none of them were that serious. Krista liked her life on her own terms.'

'I'd noticed,' I said.

Guy came in from the garden to loudly announce that he had an appointment, and had to leave. Olivia said she could give me only another hour because she had to be elsewhere too. I decided to confine my search today to just the study. Maybe I could arrange with Olivia to come back another day to do the methodical grind of checking the pocket of every coat, removing every book from the shelf, talking to the neighbours. I was not enthusiastic. It was a myth that the police were not thorough. They weren't always bright, but they were usually very thorough. In a high-profile case like this, a contract killing in a public place, they would be ultra-thorough and unlikely to leave even the shadow of a clue to be found by an ex-journalist who looks in his bathroom mirror and sees Philip Marlowe.

Olivia asked if I'd like more coffee. I said I would, just to give her something to do. While she was in the kitchen, I started to look through the drawers of Krista's desk. There wasn't much, just the stuff the police had rejected. A few magazines, stationary, a sheaf of invitations to exhibitions, a pale blue cardboard folder containing some correspondence. There were a dozen or so letters, giving an instant snapshot of the daily life of a rich young woman. One was from a firm of landscape gardeners giving an estimate for some work. Another was something about a planned college reunion, a livery stable was notifying her of an increase in its charges, a sculpture gallery was inviting her to a private preview. And a firm of solicitors was enquiring about the sale of a painting.

Sale of a painting? I looked at the letter again. I was sure it was the same firm of solicitors that had written to Marjorie more than a year ago. I seemed to recognise the distinctive headed notepaper. They were based near Manchester, and their letter was dated two months ago. It said they were acting for a client who was an art collector and who was particularly interested in paintings by the portrait artist Seymour Stackford. It was understood that Miss Carlton had such a painting, and was she prepared to sell? Their client, they added pointedly, was prepared to pay 'well above market value' due to his particular interest in this artist.

I walked into the big bright yellow-painted kitchen, where Olivia was rinsing cups and put the direct question. 'What happened to the painting, the one by Seymour Stackford, the one someone wanted to buy?'

'It's still in storage, with a lot more of Marjorie's stuff we never had room for. Before she lost her sight, she lived in a very large house, and when her husband died and she moved here. She was our favourite aunt and we wanted to look after her. When she moved, she had a lot of things and she didn't want to part with most of the them. She and Bernard, her husband, had had a long and happy life together, and her possessions held too many memories, I think. We tried to persuade her to have a clear out, but in the end they were all put into storage.'

'So Krista didn't sell it after she inherited?'

'No, I don't think so. She wouldn't have disposed of any of

Marjorie's things without offering them to us first.'

'What's so special about the painting?' I asked.

'Nothing really.' She paused while she carefully poured milk into the coffee, and then handed me the cup. 'The picture was a gift from Bernard to Majorie in the 1940s, not long after they'd met. It's been years since I saw it. It just shows a young man and woman, they were meant to be a couple I suppose, standing together. I think I recall Bernard saying he bought it a saleroom on a whim because he said the girl in the picture looked exactly like Marjorie. He liked to make romantic gestures. I suppose that's why she never wanted to part with it.'

'Is it valuable? Some old paintings can be worth a fortune.'

Olivia shrugged. 'Not this one. We did have it valued once, but we were told it was worth just a few hundred pounds. The artist wasn't one of those who is highly regarded. He didn't make any sort of name for himself.'

It wasn't the answer I wanted. People will kill for a million-pound painting, and I could have been onto something. But two contract killings for a picture worth a few hundred? I didn't think so. And I carried on not thinking so for a couple of minutes. The one thing you became as a journalist was cynical, and after the two minutes were up, the instinct that dominated my old job told me that when somebody offers more than something is worth, they usually have a reason different from the one that is actually given. Back at Krista's desk, I jotted down the name, address and telephone number of the law firm.

The more I thought about it, the more I convinced myself it could be a lead. When read separately, the letters meant nothing, just part of the microcosm of family business. And the police had read them separately - and months apart. In fact, it was likely different officers were involved too. No reason to make a connection.

But read together, the two letters revealed... well, nothing specific, just a certain persistence on the part of the writer. It was the nearest thing to a clue that a clueless detective had, and I grasped at it. I felt there might possibly be a connection between the interest in the painting and the execution of Marjorie and Krista and that meant I had to find out the name of person that the solicitors were acting for.

Back at base, I flicked through the boxes containing Marjorie's life and times until I found the letter enquiring about the painting. It was from the same firm of solicitors as the letter sent to Krista. A further shuffle through the paperwork also turned up something else I recalled seeing, a note from the original valuer, describing the artist as 'of no significance'. Attached to this note was a colour photograph of the painting. It showed a young couple standing close together in a country-garden setting. The pose was rather stiff and formal, though if you looked closely, you could see that the man's arm was actually around the woman's waist, his hand just visible on her left hip. It was a pleasant enough painting, but rather ordinary. I slipped the photo in my pocket.

Then I reached for the telephone. It was time to make something happen.

Doyle, Dakyn, and Dunn were a firm of solicitors based in Wilmslow, a wealthy area in the Cheshire countryside south of Manchester. Lawyers were a tight-minded bunch at the best of times, and I knew the chances of getting the name of a client from them was so remote it fell into the waste of time category. But I'd got no other tangible leads, so I rang up and made an appointment to see Mr Dakyn, whose scrawling signature was above the typewritten name on the letter to Marjorie.

His secretary didn't like the fact that I wouldn't specify the nature of the matter to be discussed, but I didn't like her tone much either, so that evened it out. I said Mr Dakyn had been recommended to me, the matter was highly confidential and any other details would have to be for his ears only. She made the appointment with as little as enthusiasm as she could muster, and I had this distinct feeling that she was mentally adding a zero to the consultancy bill, just because of my irritation quotient.

I spent the two days between that telephone call and the actual appointment doing little more than rearrange the items on my desk while I sat aimlessly rotating in my swivel chair. However I came at the problem, all directions were as featureless as a white-out blizzard. The one constructive thing I did was telephone the only art expert I knew. Jeremy Le Roye worked for a firm of regional auctioneers, based in one of the nicer parts of Birmingham. Actually to be in one of the nicer parts of Birmingham you need to be well out of Birmingham, and his big Georgian terraced office was so far west along the Hagley Road it was virtually in open countryside. I had met him a couple of times in the past, when I was based in the Midlands writing newspaper features, and we got on well enough for me to give him a call to beg a favour. He was a tall, thin, almost skeletal man who looked just the way you'd expect a deranged art expert to look, wiry grey stand-on-end hair, half-moon glasses and the biggest collection of vibrant bow-ties you'd get this side of the Annual Bow-Tie Makers Ball.

I didn't give him any of the background, just said I'd be interested to know if painting by a particular artist had any significant value. 'Can't say I've heard of that one,' he said when I pushed the name Seymour Stackford his way. 'Don't worry, I've got all the books so leave it with me and I'll have a scan through and get back to you.'

By the time I started the four hour drive up to Wilmslow for my meeting with Dakyn I still hadn't heard anything from Jeremy so I set off for the meeting not only holding no ace cards, but no cards at all. Still, playing it by ear is one of my strong points.

In Wilmslow, the main street was a showcase for trendy bars and bistros, boutiques and estate agents. It did not take me long to spot Doyle, Dakyn and Dunn. They had a bold fascia sign with silver serif letters on a black background. A car was just vacating a parking space right outside their tall black-painted double doors, and I slid my Mercedes into it, hoping that this tiny piece of luck would be a good omen for the meeting.

Through the black doors there was a polished wooden floor, black leather and chrome furniture, and a semi-circular reception desk. Behind the desk was a girl who looked to be in her early twenties. Her face was stark white, her lips had the gloss of black cherries, and her short dark hair had an inch-wide alien red streak down one side. She wore a black tailored jacket, high buttoned, and no jewellery. Miss White Face reeled off a mechanical 'How can I help you?' greeting, and when I told her I had an appointment, she pointed me to a row of four low leather seats while she picked up the telephone and said 'There is a Mr Slater to see you.' She didn't even look at me when she said: 'Please wait until you are called.'

I wasn't expecting much from the meeting, so I'd set my mind to disappointment mode. Dakyn was about seventy, thin and aluminium-haired and he looked like that dapper old actor Wilfred Hyde White, but without the jovial smile. His office was painted icy blue and displayed much black leather and dark mahogany. It was bleak and impersonal, and so was Dakyn.

Although as an unknown new client, I could have been a multi-millionaire about to place a massive amount of business his way, he was curt and matter-of-fact and unwelcoming. He simply asked me to state my business. He had a notepad open on his desk, and a fountain pen in his right hand. I was just four words into the conversation when he put the pen down. All I'd said was 'I'm a private detective' and his interest was terminated. He didn't actually say anything, but I could almost see the perma-frost edging across the desk towards me. I explained I was investigating the murder of Marjorie Wilkes, that there was correspondence between Mrs Wilkes and his unnamed client and it was essential to the investigation that I was able to contact his client who may have vital information that could help solve this horrific case, which I am sure he recalled reading about at the time it occurred.

Dakyn closed his notepad with scarcely-coded finality and stood up. He said that unless there was a direct request from the police for such information, then client confidentiality had to be paramount. 'I can pass your request to my client, but whether or not he responds is up to him. He is a very busy man and travels a great deal.'

That was a definite no. Otherwise it wouldn't have been necessary to bother adding the busy-man-travelling stuff. Dakyn was already walking towards the door, pointedly showing me out. I wanted to make some barbed and witty comment, but I decided to retain my dignity and left. The fact that I couldn't think of anything barbed and witty to say may have had something to do with it. As I glanced over my shoulder to close the door behind me, he had already turned his back and was flicking through the folders in a filing cabinet. That was when I had the idea.

I realised that the information I needed was very likely to be in one of those filing cabinets. We might be in the age of technology but lawyers liked lots of paper. They still wrote to people. They didn't like emails – you couldn't charge so much for them. There was a row of three cabinets and if only I had a few minutes alone, I could quickly search the files. It was obvious that to guarantee being alone in that office, I would need to pick exactly the right time. About 3am.

The obvious problem was the office would not be open then, and that I was not a burglar. But you don't spend twenty years being a journalist without knowing a man who is.

Alexander Charlton Evans was never called Alexander or Charlton or even Alex or Charlie. He was called Ace, ever since we saw that was what his initials spelled when he biro'd them onto his plastic pencil case at junior school. Back then, Ace, Trevor, the Clarke twins Paul and Phil, and of course me, were all pals, and hung around together, and it stayed that way through senior school too. Then we split up and everyone went to college except Ace, who just went wrong.

We kept in touch because we had all lived in the same

neighbourhood, but Ace had chosen a different path and seemed to enjoy it. He was in juvenile court for a bit of shoplifting, a bit of vandalism, and by the time he was nineteen, he got a three-year stretch for burglary. When he came out, it was evident that he had learned a lot. Mainly how not to get caught. By then I was in journalism and our paths crossed occasionally as I used him as a good source of information and background material. It always cost me the odd fifty quid, but it was usually worth it. These days, I only had a vague idea of what Ace was all about. Whatever it was he had done quite well, for when I last met him a few months earlier he was driving a new Audi A6 and he assured me it wasn't stolen. But he hinted with a wry smile that he was still 'in the same business' as he put it. He had obviously just got better at it.

I turned the car into a layby and scrolled up Ace's number on my phone. He answered immediately and after a brief exchange of old-days banter, we arranged to meet in an hour in a pub by junction 13 of the M6. I was still musing about the old days as I nosed the Mercedes through heavy traffic back down the motorway.

Ace looked well. He had gelled hair and a thin neatly-shaved goatee beard that looked like it had been stencilled on with a felt-tipped pen. He wore smart casual clothes and he still had the black Audi. He seemed genuinely glad to see me, or was at least faking it well.

The pub was almost empty and there was no one sitting near us but we still spoke in a guarded way. I said I knew some premises that were difficult to access and could he help. He wanted more details and when I told him it was a solicitors' office, I think he rather liked the idea. He said that as it was me asking, he would do it as a favour – plus a grand in cash. 'How much would it have been without the favour?' I asked.

'Probably wouldn't do it at all,' he said. 'I've moved onto other things now. I don't do much direct work anymore, I'm more into management.' The wry smile told me he was probably now a fence, running a profitable steal-to-order racket, with a small team of hand-picked 'associates' to do the risky stuff.

'Still, as it's you, and as I loathe lawyers, and as now and again I like to keep my hand in...' He left the sentence unfinished and I knew the arrangement was in place. Outside, I gave him the address and there was a brief discussion of details. It had to be a joint operation because while he could get in, he couldn't find what I wanted. I had to carry out the search myself. His confidence in his talents gave me confidence. He said whatever the security system was, it was unlikely to present him with a problem. He also planned to gain access at around 11pm which I thought was much too early. I voiced my doubts but he shook his head and laughed.

'That's why you're not in this business,' he said. 'Best way not to be seen is to be about when there are lots of people around, and at that time it'll be busy with people coming out of the pubs. On a deserted street, you'll always be seen slipping into an alley. When it's busy, you're invisible.' He shook my hand, and slapped me on the shoulder. 'Don't worry,' he said. 'I'll look after you.'

He seemed keen to show me that he made the right career choice in life, and that my better academic prowess from my school days had not been such an advantage. Just like at school, he enjoyed being the centre of attention, and I rather felt he was looking forward to demonstrating his skills to an old classmate. The old classmate was already getting rather nervy. If this little project went wrong, Ace and I would be spending a lot of time together in the near future, probably three to five years. I liked him, but not that much.

Next night I stood in a bar in Wilmslow waiting for Ace and I felt like having a stiff drink for I was uneasy to the point of being scared. I would have liked a large vodka but I had to drive back. I then realised I was about to commit a burglary yet was worrying about a drink-driving offence. I ordered the vodka.

At about 10.30pm Ace breezed in, relaxed and smiling,

and his jaunty manner helped reassure me. He had already scouted the premises and told me they ranked only 4 on his 0-10 scale of access-difficulty. While the imposing offices of Doyle, Dakyn and Dunn fronted a busy main street, the rear of the building was just a small walled yard. A padlocked iron gate had been no obstacle, the alarm system, although a good one, was a few years old, and all-too-easy for Ace to disable. His check also revealed there was no CCTV. A small pane had been removed from one of the Georgian-style windows and the window lock overcome with some little multi-purpose tool that was apparently always the number one choice on the novice burglar's Christmas wants-list.

The walled courtyard screened me as I rather inelegantly clambered through the now-open window, and I was on my own, heart pounding. Ace had ambled off, job done, brown envelope in his pocket, and was presently cruising back towards the M6. He had resisted all pleadings to nurse-maid me. 'There's a limit to how much risk I'll take for a grand,' he said, grinning at my obvious unease. 'You'll be OK. Just be quick.' He patted my shoulder reassuringly, and left.

So now I was shuffling along towards Dakyn's office guided by the thin beam of my pocket torch. Ace had checked the doors between the rear window and the target office and none were locked. And that was also the case with the filing cabinets. 'Even lawyers get complacent,' he said with a faint smile.

Three filing cabinets, each with three drawers, dozens of folders, and a wavering torch light. This could take some time. The cabinets were full of A–Z name listings and of course, I didn't know the name I was looking for. I spent about 10 minutes randomly burrowing through the folders when I noticed one headed Overseas Clients. Dakyn had let slip that the mystery client travelled a lot. So maybe he was based abroad. It was a slim folder, which suggested the firm didn't have many overseas clients, so it wouldn't take long to check.

The first letters I saw were the ones I wanted.

Now you could say I was lucky, but I think you make your own luck, and I'd made things happen just by being there. The first letter was the initial instruction to the law firm. It referred to the matter as 'commercially sensitive' and emphasised the need for the client's identity not to be divulged in any circumstances. There was an interesting and telling paragraph, stating 'that no expense was to be spared in the pursuit of the objective and there was no need to consult regarding any expenditure.' In short, it was making clear this was a blank-cheque venture, ensuring total dedication of the lawyer by implying that high fees could be charged without question. Neat touch.

Scanning the rest of the letters, I noted they were to-and-fro correspondence reporting on the refusal of Marjorie Wilkes to sell the painting, despite repeated approaches. The final letter in the series instructed the lawyer to inform Mrs Wilkes that she could name 'a six figure sum' for the painting. Attached was a copy of the Dakyn's reply, stating that despite his best endeavours Mrs Wilkes was not interested in selling, due to the sentimental value of the painting to her.

The final two letters concerned Krista. Similar approaches, identical refusal to sell the picture, despite a potential big offer. I suppose it's easy to say no when you already have a few million.

The client's name was Kirkland Ryan and he had a company called Unique World Business Index. But I wasn't much interested in his name or his company at that moment. I was more interested in the address. The company was based in Los Angeles. That was very important, because the USA was the kind of place to buy shoes.

Black slip-on shoes with a tiny brass motif shaped like a rodeo rider.

4

The pilot smacked the plane onto the runway at Los Angeles airport as if he was exploring the outer limits of the tyre pressures. The reverse-thrust braking jerked me forward and focussed my thoughts. Throughout the tedious flight I felt decidedly out of place among the other passengers, mainly holiday makers dressed in offensively bright clothes and with screaming, demanding children. I had tried to shut myself off, trying to read, trying to sleep, moodily sipping water and ignoring the conversational attempts of the plump, shiny-faced woman next to me. Now and then I had tried to decide what I would do once I arrived in LA. It was not a productive exercise. I'd left the UK with no plan, a hasty, throw-some-clothes-into-a-holdall departure with lots of intent and no forethought. Now, as the plane was being parked, I realised just how stupid this was. I registered the fact, then cleared my mind and reminded myself of just why I had decided I had to come to LA.

Once I had melted away from the scene of the law firm burglary, my first thought was to research Unique World Business Index. Even as I put the files back in the cabinet, closed them and backtracked, shutting all the doors behind me, I was already picturing endless hours on the internet and telephone trying to put together some sort of dossier on the firm and Mr Kirkland Ryan as I unhurriedly walked along the alley way behind Dakyn's offices and mingled with crowds still coming out of the bars. Of course the break-in would be reported, but as nothing had been stolen, I couldn't see how the incident could be connected with that particular client, or to me.

Driving back down the motorway, I was feeling pleased at making even a little progress but then I got a call from Jeremy Le Roye.

'Sorry Max, I know it's a bit late but I tried to get you earlier. I haven't got any good news for you. The artist isn't anybody of note. Seems he made a living in the late 1800s mainly doing portraits for the wealthy, but he did no exhibition work, and made no great name for himself. His work is quite routine and of no significant value. The last picture I can trace being sold was a couple of years ago. It fetched four hundred pounds in an auction in London.'

I thanked Jeremy for his research and even as I touched the off button, his answer had posed a new question - why was Kirkland Ryan prepared to pay a six-figure sum for a painting worth next to nothing? Whatever the reason it had already cost two lives, and I owed it to Krista Carlton, and old Marjorie, to uncover the truth. I could still see Krista, perched elegantly on the edge of a chair in my office just a few days ago. What was it she said? 'I chose you because you have so much to prove.' So I started packing a bag.

LA airport looked like most international airports, just acres of numbing functionality, an almost designless structure seemingly intended to further depress tired travellers. Dodging through the fat women, wayward trolleys and untamed children, I headed for the car-hire desks, choosing the one with the shortest queue and co-incidentally, the rudest attendant. I handed over my credit card in exchange for a Chrysler, which from the curt directions, seemed to be parked about three miles away

It was almost five o'clock in the afternoon, but when I stepped outside the building to locate the parking bay, there was still sufficient heat to do toast if you held it close enough to the pavement. It was a dirty, gritty heat, the air heavy and over-used. As I trekked to find the car, I was recalling the Steve Martin movie Trains, Planes And Automobiles, the scene where he struggled through snow to reach his numbered bay, only to find it empty. But it was not an omen. In Bay 267 there was a dusty metallic-green Chrysler which fired up immediately and I headed out to the highway, turning north towards Santa Monica. There, a journalist friend, Terry Leonard had a house, and I had arranged to borrow it. Terry used to work for The Times in London but eight years earlier had moved to California after he married an American girl he met in a bar in Carnaby Street. He'd started freelancing and had built up a good business feeding quirky stateside stories to the British media. When I had called him to ask if I could stay with at his house, I found he was over in London on vacation, so he arranged for me to pick up a set of keys from his neighbour.

'What about Karen?' I asked. 'Will she mind?'

'She lives in Bakersfield with a truck driver she met. We lasted just four months.'

Santa Monica is only about ten miles from the airport, so the fact that there was a black Toyota in my rear view mirror the whole time didn't register at all. When I turned off Highway 10, looping right onto Lincoln Boulevard, the Toyota followed. As I took another right onto Olympic, it was still there. And when, a few minutes and a couple of wrong turns later, I found Pico Street, a neat estate of white palm-fringed bungalows where Terry lived, the Toyota pulled up a little way behind me. I still hadn't noticed it.

I noticed it soon afterwards though.

As I got out of my car and closed the door, there was just a half second glimpse of the Toyota hurtling at me, tyres screaming for traction as the driver floored the pedal. You don't take in a lot in half a second. The Toyota smacked into me as I stood frozen at the side of my Chrysler. There was a momentary spasm of searing pain and I hit the ground hard. I felt dazed but immediately I knew I was dead. There was an angel in front of me dressed in blinding white. She was swirling and fuzzy with no sharp definitions. She was young and had golden hair and was reaching out to touch me. I was thankful there was a heaven and glad I was in it and glad there were angels. There was no doubt she was an angel because as my vision sharpened I saw that she had the word Angel in large black letters floating in front of her. They were a moving wavy line, the letters curving gently up and over snowy white mountain peaks.

I blinked. I blinked again. They were not mountain peaks. They were breasts. The angel was wearing a tight white T-shirt that had the word ANGEL printed large across the chest. I was lying flat on my back on the pavement. There was a lot of pain from my left hip and leg, and I could feel blood trickling into my left eye. Several people were kneeling over me holding me down. Someone had put a coat or something under my head and a blanket over me. Someone else had dialled 911. I wasn't sure which bits of me I might still be able to move and I was rather afraid to try. I lay still, and in minutes a distant siren grew ever closer, and soon an ambulance pulled up and medics were out and tending me. The Angel had disappeared.

The next couple of hours were tiresome for me, and tiresome to relate. The good news was that I was not seriously injured. The bad news was that I hurt like hell. It appeared I had subconsciously given my body a half turn to flatten myself against the Chrysler as the Toyota leapt at me. Instead of slamming into me full on and sending me tumbling under its wheels, the Toyota had hit me a hard glancing blow that had sent me spinning like a top. I had a severely bruised hip and thigh, and an inch-long cut along the line of my left eyebrow, where I had hit the road surface. It had been a very lucky escape. After the tests and X-rays, they dressed my cuts and scuffs and allowed me to go. Once I'd given them my credit card of course. I took a taxi back to the bungalow, searched for the drinks cupboard and poured myself a triple vodka. It went down in one.

Physically, I felt battered. Mentally, I was struggling to stay sharp. Oddly, I was absolutely obsessed with one thing, and it should have been the Toyota. But it wasn't. It was the Angel. Who was she? I had to know. Twenties. Blonde. Grey eyes. White Angel T-shirt. That's all I knew. The medication and the vodka started to hit me hard and I flopped onto the bed with the vision of the Angel floating above me.

Sometime later a strange shrill sound woke me and it took a minute to realise it was probably a telephone. My left leg felt stiff as an ironing board and I did a fast comic shuffle to get to the phone before it stopped ringing. It was Boyd Prevost, a local freelance journalist Terry had recommended. 'Boyd knows everyone and everything,' he'd told me. 'Hiring him will save you a lot of time.'

Before I left the UK, I had contacted Boyd and asked him to call me, briefly explaining I was researching a magazine feature, and would pay him his usual daily rate for some assistance. Now, he was calling to set up a meeting. He suggested we meet up that night, at about 9pm at the Tropical Bar on the beach front on Pacific Avenue, and gave me directions. I made some coffee, eased myself into an armchair and decided to concentrate on what lay ahead, formulate some sort of plan. Within minutes, I was asleep.

It was about 7pm when I woke, the sun low but still bright. I was still moving like a man of 90 but my head was clear and I was eager for action. Taking a shower helped loosen me up a little, and some tinned food - all I could find in the bungalow - boosted me too. I was ready to face the evening, get some enquiries underway. The process would start with my briefing Boyd, and I set out to meet him with optimism.

It was difficult to miss the Tropical Bar. It was long and open-fronted, with dwarf palms in wooden barrels symmetrically placed. There was loud music and a young clientele made up mostly of shaven-headed guys and skimpy-topped girls failing to find the right balance between trash and class.The bar had a couple of large blue and yellow illuminated globes rotating above it that acted like beacons drawing in those who wanted exotic cocktails that looked like the colour of cleaning fluid. The bar faced the sea, but there was a busy road between it and the beach, and the on-street parking was bumper to scraped bumper. I was finally able to slot the Chrysler into a tight space a couple of hundred metres down the road and started my inelegant stiff-legged shuffle back towards the Tropical. The street was packed with people looking as if they were having a better time that I was. Just before the Tropical was another bar, same sort of crowd, different name. At a table pavement table a pretty waitress was putting down a tray of drinks.

It was the Angel.

For just a moment she didn't recognise me, then the grazed cheekbone and the stitching in my eyebrow registered and she said 'It's you! The guy who almost got himself killed.'

I nodded. 'That's me. I want to thank you. What's your name?'

'Nikki. Are you English?'

'Yes, just arrived in LA. I'm Max'.

She was about five feet five, slim but still curvy. Her hair was just cut straight and simple to shoulder length. Her pale skin showed just the faintest tan, as if she hadn't been in the sun too much, and her eyes were light grey. She wore a top just a fraction bigger than a bikini, with string-like shoulder straps. It was some sort of leopard print shot with faint silver flecks. Her midriff was bare and her tiny puckered belly button was pierced with a curved silver clip with a heart shaped green stone on the lower arc. The short tight black skirt displayed most of her legs and her shoes were simple black and flat heeled.

I looked up at her face. 'Seen enough?' she said, all too aware of my searching appraisal. She had a soft confident voice. Her lips were perfect and pouting and they were the kind of lips which suggested if they kissed you, they would leave a lingering memory.

'Sorry, but you're quite a distraction,' I said. 'Thanks for helping out last night. It could have been worse. At least I'm still alive.'

'It was no accident,' she said. 'He just drove straight at you.'

'I don't know,' I said, 'I'd only been in America about ten minutes. Maybe he was just a bad driver. Either way, I'd really like to thank you properly. Can I buy you a drink later?'

She shook her head. 'I'm working,' she said.

'Tomorrow night?'

'I work every night.'

'Take a night off,' I suggested.

'Can't. I need the money.'

'I just want the opportunity to say thanks properly. It would mean a lot to me.'

She was wavering, but probably only while she thought of another way of saying no.

Tell you what,' I added, not giving her chance to refuse. I pointed to a pizza restaurant next door. 'Take a few minutes off, come and have a coffee over there with me, and I'll give you $200. Let's call it a thank-you present. This is absolutely on the level.' I was shocked at my own persistence.

The offer threw her, fazed her into an uncertain silence. I'd definitely succeeded in getting her attention, but for how long? Nikki looked back at me and gave me the same kind of once-over stare I'd given her minutes earlier. She saw a tall slim guy who hoped he still passed for 35 giving her the best smile he could muster with a badly grazed cheekbone.

'Are all you English guys this crazy?' she said. 'Let me get it straight. You give me $200 to have a coffee with you where everybody can see us, right?

'Right,' I said.

'Cash up front?'

'Right now,' I said, dipping into my pocket and pulling out the money. I peeled off the bills and handed them to her.

'Okay. It's your money. I'm due a break in 20 minutes. I'll

see you then.'

'Great,' I said. 'Don't change your mind.'

As she left, I was already shaking my head at what I had just done. Maybe it was the bizarre way we had met, with me semi-conscious on the sidewalk, maybe the pain-killers had loosened my inhibitions, but I had really fallen for her. I felt a weird connection, as if fate had intervened. Or perhaps my head had taken a harder knock than I thought. Either way, the surprising thing was she had agreed to meet up so I was going to run with the situation.

I walked as briskly as I could to the Tropical next door where I quickly found Boyd. The picture on his website had shown him to be tall, gaunt, early forties and badly in need of a haircut. I recognised him immediately, seated at a table by the entrance, smoking a small cigar and eyeing up a big broad-shouldered brunette perched on a tall stool. She was wearing an almost non-existent skirt.

I apologised for being late. 'No problem,' he said, nodding in the direction of the big brunette. 'Nice scenery while I wait.'

Explaining I was pressed for time and needed to be brief, I launched into a terse explanation of what I wanted him to do. I didn't tell him about the killings of Marjorie and Krista. There was no need at this stage to over-complicate things. I just said I'd been commissioned by a British magazine to dig the dirt on Kirkland Ryan, who was suspected of fraud. I told him to devote as much time as he could to the matter and as soon as he could, report back to me. I gave him my mobile number. Boyd said he hadn't heard of Ryan or Unique World Business Index but he'd start checking and get back to me. We exchanged a few pleasantries, he assured me he'd get started next day. I left him still hoping he was going to get lucky with the girl on the bar stool.

The pain in my leg was beginning to ease a little and although there was a persistent ache from my ribs too, I didn't feel that bad overall. I found an empty table on the pavement outside the pizzeria and waited. Nikki could have kept the money and not showed up but five minutes later she strolled across.

I noticed she'd changed her top to one which was equally small, but scarlet with a silver lightning flash across the front. Was that a positive sign? She'd clearly thought enough about our meeting to get changed. Either that or that someone had spilled a drink over her.

'Hi,' she said, sitting opposite me. Did you think I wouldn't show?'

'Maybe'.

'If you were really a wacko, you wouldn't have suggested meeting here. Too crowded.'

'Good point.'

'I don't get you,' she said, leaning forward and resting her elbows on the small circular table. 'Like most waitresses, I get hit on a lot, but this is the first time a guy has offered to pay me $200 to have a cup of coffee with him.' Her eyes narrowed. 'And just because I'm here, don't get any wrong ideas. I'm not for hire for anything else.'

'Good.' I said. 'Because if you were for hire for anything else, I wouldn't want to be with you. So now do we understand each other?'

She was staring at me, still uncertain.

We ordered cappuccinos and I told her that when I was lying on the pavement barely consciousness, I really had thought she was an angel, and she laughed. And the more I told her about how I was visualising that wavy word angel gliding over her breasts the more she laughed. Her initial uneasiness was dissipating and we chatted for ten minutes or so about little or nothing and seemed to be getting on well. So I pushed my luck.

'Can I ask you a personal question?' I said.

'How personal?'

'Very personal.'

She was looking intrigued. 'Try me,' she said.
'Are you in love?'

'What!'

'Simple question. Are you in love?'

'I'm seeing a guy.'

'That's not what I asked. Seeing someone doesn't mean you're in love, it just means you're seeing someone. It means you might be in love one day, but not right now.'

She was looking a little uneasy.

'Here's the test,' I said, trying to do a Tom Cruise charm smile. 'Can you bear to be away from him even for a few hours? Do you feel breathless when he walks into the room? Does your heart beat quicker when you're alone with him?

She was looking worried. I held her stare and then said slowly 'Because if you don't feel all of those things, you're not in love. If you can look directly into my eyes, and tell me you are in love, then I promise I'll go away. But if you're just seeing someone…'

I let the sentence trail away. Her hesitancy and confusion told me unmistakably that she wasn't in love. She was toying with her spoon, aimlessly stirring the coffee. At least she hadn't got up and walked away.

Nikki stopped stirring the coffee and put the spoon back on the saucer. Her eyes were bright.

'You are one crazy guy,' she said, her face faintly flushed.

'Usually, I can read guys but it's tough with you. I don't know if you're just different, or just weird.'

'That means you need more time with me to find out.'

She got up. 'I've got to go,' she said tersely.

I pushed another $200 across the table, fanning the notes like playing cards.

She looked puzzled, as she was meant to.

'What's that for? You paid me in advance.'

'It's for having lunch with me tomorrow.'

'You are crazy, aren't you?' she said.

I nodded.

A waiter came past and she asked if she could borrow his pen. She scribbled on a paper napkin and handed it to me. 'That's my cellphone number,' she said. 'Call me tomorrow. But make it after lunch. I work at the bar until two, so I sleep late.'

She turned away, walking quickly and not looking back. I watched until the very last flash of blondeness was lost in the crowd. She had left the money on the table.

Suddenly, I felt very tired. I made my way to the Chrysler and easy my aching body onto the seat. Easing out into the traffic, I turned right towards Pico Street and my welcoming bed. One thing I don't do is learn quickly. It may have been tiredness or just carelessness, but I didn't notice that the headlights in my rear view mirror were the same ones all the way back, or that the car they were on stopped twenty metres behind me when I pulled up outside the bungalow.

It took me a moment to slide the key into the lock and push the front door open and before I could even find the light switch, I was shoved violently from behind and went skittling down the hallway, crashing into a table before bouncing against the kitchen door. The door flew open and I slid along the tiled floor. My assailant piled on top of me pinning down my arms with his knees and then leaning forward. There was some faint light filtering into the kitchen from a street lamp outside, just enough for me to see the face of the man with a shaven head and thin lips drawn back in a snarl of glinty white teeth. There was enough light for me to see he had four gold studs in his left ear. I counted them. I had nothing else to do.

He hit me hard across the face, not a punch, but with the back of his hand. The power of the blow flicked my head to the right. Still kneeling on my arms, he leaned back slightly, reaching behind him. I couldn't see what he had in his hand but I soon discovered it was a knife. I could feel the cold sharp tip of the steel cutting through my chinos in the spot I least wanted a very sharp knife to be.

Between my legs.

5

It's always a good idea to keep perfectly still when someone has a knife touching your balls and in any event, when a fifteen-stone gorilla is pinning you to the floor you don't have much choice. I did nothing except breathe quietly and I hoped inoffensively. The gorilla twitched the blade of the knife a little just to remind me that it was there. He leaned forward, his dark silhouette blotting out the rest of my vision.

'Listen good,' he said. 'I saw you with her. She's mine, so stay away from her. Got that?' His weight on my chest was beginning to squeeze the air from my lungs.

'Understood.' It's always wise to agree with everything a man with a knife says.

In one way I was quite relieved because I realised the guy with the knife wasn't a hitman about to kill me. He was obviously the guy Nikki was seeing. I was going to have to speak to her about her choice in men. She could do better.

'Don't fucking forget it.'

His weight lifted off me and he backed away, lost in the darkness. I heard his footfall cross the hallway and then there was silence. I got to my feet and switched on all the lights. In the bathroom mirror, my face looked like it had come from a meat counter. I had started the day with a stitched eyebrow and a grazed cheek. Now my left cheek was swollen, my lip was bleeding and the blood had spread all over my chin. I splashed on cold water, cleaned myself up, and then went to find the vodka. I sat down in an armchair, drinking from the bottle. My hand wasn't too steady and I admitted to myself I'd been scared. I also felt bad about not putting up any sort of fight but I believed discretion was the better part of valour. All cowards believe that.

But there was a surprising upside to the incident. If that was Nikki's guy, then it might not be such a tall order to convince her I would be a better option. I wasn't built like the gorilla but I knew I could be much considerate.

It could have been the vodka I suppose, but it was noon before I woke up, and only then because my face felt so hot. The sun was slanting through the open curtains branding a burning rectangle onto my pillow. The bathroom mirror told me the swelling on my cheeks had subsided, and with the flesh less sore, I washed off the remainder of the dried blood. In a clean shirt and with my hair combed, I looked just about passable for public viewing as long as there were no small children about.

There was no bread in the house – grocery shopping hadn't found its way to the top of my priority list - but I did find a packet of biscuits, and made some tea. Then the phone rang. It was Boyd with the results of his research. It wasn't much. All he could tell me about the World Directories operation was that it published business directories which apparently circulated all over Europe, though not in the States. It seemed a legitimate business, registered to Kirkland Ryan, but he had been unable to dig up any personal information about him. The only useful information was that the company had a rented office in Hollywood, on Ivar Avenue. Boyd had also come up with Ryan's home address. He lived on the coast some 10 miles north west, near Ventura.

'I went for a drive by, and there was nothing much to see,' said Boyd. 'It's a big Spanish-style place with a swimming pool but you can't see much more. It's surrounded by a high wall and there are iron gates tall enough for a castle. I yanked the bell-pull a few times, on the pretext of asking directions, but nobody came. But I did notice an interesting sign on the gates.'

'What did it say?'

'It didn't need to say anything,' he said. 'It was a picture of a Doberman.'

'Thanks for the warning. Being bitten by a big dog is just about the only thing that hasn't happened to me so far. But then I've only been here for one day.'

I thanked Boyd and told him I'd call him when I needed him again. It seemed the next step was to go to Ryan's office. I reminded myself that in the movies, visiting the villain seldom turned out to be a wise thing to do. Yet I knew I was going to do it anyway, because I couldn't think of anything else to do. I opened up a street map of LA, and searched for Ivar Avenue. The name seemed oddly familiar and then it came to me. It was in the heart of Philip Marlowe territory. Marlowe had an office in the Cahuenga Building on Hollywood Boulevard. I scanned the map with a mild frisson of excitement. I was in LA, in Marlowe's backyard, investigating murder. How much closer than you get to your fictional hero? There it was, Cahuenga Boulevard, bisecting Sunset and Hollywood. And running parallel was Ivar Avenue, my destination.

The sky was infinity blue, the temperature rising. As I got into my Chrysler the heat was unbearable. I set the air-con to maximum and gave it a minute to have some effect before looping that car around and joining the Santa Monica Boulevard to follow its length straight into the heart of Hollywood. Mid-morning traffic was tolerable and moved steadily. I passed street signs I'd read so often in Raymond Chandler's novels: Le Brea, Highland, finally Vine, and seeing that one meant I had overshot my turn while in my Marlowe dream-world. I drove up Vine and close to its junction with Hollywood Boulevard, saw a sign saying GREAT PARKING, and below, rather oddly, 'SINCE 1929'. Could parking actually be 'great?' Or improve with age?

I left the car and found myself at a famous crossroads. In decades past, Hollywood and Vine was a glitzy junction where movie stars and moguls could be seen cruising by in flashy Studebakers or elegant Rolls Royces, or even walking to lunch dates at the renowned Brown Derby restaurant. Now, all that glamour was gone. It was just another car-clogged intersection. The beautiful people had moved on to newly-fashionable parts of town.

Google map in hand, I glanced around. To my right a couple of blocks distant I could see the Capitol Records Tower, looking like a giant stack of 45s, which was precisely the intention of the two men who came up with the idea in the 1950s, not architects but singer Nat King Cole and songwriter Johnny Mercer. I made a mental note to try to view it at night. I'd heard the pulsating light on its pinnacle flashed HOLLYWOOD in Morse-code, and I wanted to check.

I started walking south and after a few blocks and a left turn found myself on Ivar Avenue, outside the Legrande Building, where Kirkland Ryan apparently based his dubious business empire. The three-story building was faced in pale grey stone, the lower frontage darkened glass which reflected the street. The mirror image showed me looking purposeful, younger than I was, and more modest.

I felt far from Philip Marlowe entering the Sternwood mansion in The Big Sleep, smartly dressed because he was 'calling on four million dollars'. My suit was back in England, so I was doing the best I could, wearing black chinos and a lightweight grey jacket. But at least my T-shirt was Armani. It has been a present from a girlfriend. Two weeks later, we split up, but I got custody of the shirt.

In the centre of the frontage were double glass doors, and on the left a neat row of name plates listing various businesses based within. The doors had large S-shaped pewter-finished handles. I pushed one, and stepped inside. The interior was light and minimalist and looked much as I anticipated. There was a wide but shallow reception room with a bleached oak floor and a few chrome-framed upright chairs with leather seats lined up against the left-hand wall. On the right there were several doors, all closed. Directly ahead of me was a curved ebony desk with the usual essential equipment - telephone, laptop, vase of fresh flowers and a blonde with a frosty attitude. She looked up with the kind of indifference you really have to practice.

'Yes?' she said with mild irritation.

'I'd like to see Mr Ryan.'

'Appointment?'

'He doesn't have to make one. I'm here already. I can see him now.'

'Do you have an appointment?' Her irritation had moved up several notches.

'No. But he might see me anyway.'

'Why is that?'

'Max Slater. I'm a private detective.' I gave her half an inch of playful smile.

'Oh.' Her perfectly structured, perfectly made-up face flushed. 'You don't look like a private detective,' she said.

'What should a detective look like?'

Miss Cool kept her hand on the telephone but didn't lift it. She looked me up and down, and then up again. 'Older, fatter, balder.'

I gave her another half inch of smile. 'You don't look like a receptionist.'

'What should a receptionist look like?'

Taking my time, I made an exaggerated pretence of looking her over.
'That would take a little while to explain,' I said, staring directly at her. 'We'd need to discuss it over a drink.'

'I don't think so.' The frost had returned. She picked up the telephone. 'Mr Ryan, a man called Max Slater wants to see you. He says he's a private detective.'

For a few seconds, she listened, then put down the receiver

unnecessarily hard. 'Mr Ryan says he doesn't know any private detectives, nor does he wish to.'

'Didn't he ask what it was about?'

'No.' She began tapping on her laptop and didn't glance up again.

Back on the street, the mid-day heat hit my face like a fist. I needed a drink and I knew exactly which one. On my left, half a block down, a red neon sign said BAR and I headed for it. Its narrow faded frontage was in a style that would pass for Victorian. Varnished dark woodwork displayed cracks and blisters and the stained glass windows hadn't been washed since Nixon was president. I went in.

The place was exactly how I wanted it to be, the sort of bar Marlowe would have used at the end of a futile day. To the right was a long shallow bar with tall shelving inset with coppered mirror panels and a sparse scattering of dull bottles. Opposite the bar was a small cluster of circular tables and armless wooden chairs. Only two tables were occupied, each by lone men clutching glasses rather too earnestly. The bar-tender glanced up from a newspaper as the door banged behind me. He was short, fat, bald and could have doubled for Danny De Vito.

'What'll you have?' he asked with minimal interest.

'Have you heard of a gimlet?'

His eyes narrowed even more as he squinted at me. 'Nobody's asked me for a gimlet for way too long. You a Chandler fan on a nostalgia trip?'

'Something like that.'

He turned away to face the murky bottles. 'Gimlet? Half gin, half lime juice. Right?'

'Rose's Lime Juice.'

'You know your Marlowe,' he grinned, spinning around with a bottle of Roses in his hand. 'This ain't been opened in a while but I guess it'll be OK.'

He set a short wide glass on the bar and poured the drink with utmost care, getting the measures as precise as he could. He was taking pride in the task. My request had leavened the dull routine of the day.

'Like one yourself?' I asked.

'Sure would', he said, sliding another glass onto the bar.

We sat sipping the thick sweet liquid without conversation. It was a bit sickly for my taste, but I was drinking as a homage to Marlowe. Apart from the muted drone of passing traffic, the bar had a church-like ambiance of tranquil meditation. Through the stained glass windows down near the entrance, a wide parallelogram of sunlight shafted in at an acute angle, dappling the floor with patches of subdued colour.

'Marlowe would have liked this bar,' I said after some minutes.

The bartender seemed pleased. 'The Long Goodbye,' he said. 'Marlowe and Terry Lennox. Late afternoon. Drinking gimlets in a bar just like this one.'

'It was called Victor's and you're keeping up the tradition,' I said. I drained my glass and slid off the stool. 'Just don't change a thing'.

I stepped from the time-vault into air almost too hot to breath. It was just after one o'clock and with my next move still to be planned, I decided to call Nikki. She responded after about twenty rings, her voice lazy and sleepy. It was going to be interesting to see whether her boyfriend had had a word with her.

'Hey, it's you,' she said, and I convinced myself she sounded pleased. 'I didn't think you'd call.'

'I didn't think you'd answer,' I said. 'You didn't seem too certain about me.'

'Still too early to be sure.' But she was laughing, which suggested that her boyfriend wasn't there, and hadn't confronted her. Maybe he thought a word with me was enough. I decided not to mention his visit for the moment.

'Can I see you later this afternoon?' I asked, pausing and then embarrassing myself by adding 'Please?' like some love-struck fool.

'Guess I'll risk it,' she said. 'I have to go into work at seven so I'll need to be back by then.'

'Any ideas where we can meet up?'

'Do you know the beach at Point Dume, just past Malibu?'

'Yes,' I lied, making a note to check my map.

'I'll see you there about two-thirty. You can park right by the sand. I'll be driving a Wrangler Jeep. It's white.'

'Never mind the colour of your car,' I said. 'I'm more interested in the colour of your bikini.'

'Who said I'll be wearing one!' It was a perfect exit line, and she was laughing as she cut the call. It was at least a minute before I put the phone down. I was using my imagination.

The sea was an intense indigo cutting a sharp line against the pale sapphire of the cloudless sky. Nikki was already there, her Jeep on the sand, the hood down and the sides feathered with dust. I parked just short of the beach and walked the last thirty metres.

She was supine on a bright pink beach towel. Despite her teasing remark, she was wearing a tiny black bikini. You could have hidden the whole thing under your wristwatch. Her hair was pulled away from her face and clipped up high, held by a tortoiseshell grip. Large sunglasses masked her eyes. She looked young and fresh and cute.

I sat on the sand beside her. I didn't think I was in bad shape. I tried to get to the gym a couple of times a week and mostly managed it. But even so I found myself drawing in my stomach a little. I was glad I had my sunglasses on too. She couldn't see the pained effort in my eyes. We spent an hour or so on insignificant conversation, a gentle lightweight exploratory series of questions and responses that allow you to get some feeling for the person, like tuning a radio. Small-talk stuff, but it erodes any awkwardness. She was from Salinas. Her father had died when she was six, and her mother was now with a man Nikki disliked, so she had left home as soon as could. She was twenty-four, liked dogs and horses and dancing, and Johnny Depp. She had worked at the beachfront bar for two years.

Initially, I asked all the questions, but then it was her turn to ask about me. I chose to give a very edited version at this stage. I didn't want to scare her, either with my past, or with my obsession for her. First off, she asked about England. Lots of questions about London. Was London like it was in the movies? 'I'd love to go there one day,' she said. Then, without preamble she asked if I was married, a direct look-you-in-the-eye question. I told myself a girl would only ask that question if she was interested in me. And then I told myself that when it came to women, I rarely knew what I was talking about.

'I was married once, but we were divorced about ten years ago. No kids, no ties, no contact anymore.'
'Why did you split?'

'I suppose that back at the start, we made the wrong choices. Or at least I did. She didn't make my heart beat faster when she came into the room.'

'Not even when you first met?'

'No. But then at that time, I was too inexperienced to know that had to happen. It's something I've learned since. The hard way. Usual heartbreak stuff.'

She was looking down at the sand, drawing circles with her fingers, and crazily, I wanted to lie to her, just say I was a journalist doing some research for a story. It would be less complicated, less scary for her. I didn't want her to know about two corpses back in the UK and the killer I was hunting. Yet because I hoped this relationship might amount to something, I didn't want to lie. So when circumstances dictate you can't lie or tell the truth, it's best to pitch the story somewhere between the two. I decided to at least be honest about my job, and I explained I was a private detective getting commercial information for a client. I didn't mention the killings.

Nikki seemed impressed, even excited about the fact I was a detective. 'Being a private eye is cool,' she said. 'I love private eye movies. Have you seen Chinatown?'

'It's one of my favourite films.'

In it, Jack Nicholson plays Jake Gittes, a flashy private eye who mostly does divorce work but gets caught up in something much darker. We started talking about old movies and I said that our chance meeting at the bar where she worked had vague echoes of Bogart meeting Ingrid Bergman in Casablanca.

'Don't think I've seen that one,' she said.

'You should, it's a classic. Let's just say he was very pleased to meet her, though he didn't show it at the time.'

'As pleased as you are to see me? I don't understand you.'

'Then why did you agree to meet me today? I can't be your type.'

'And what makes you think you know my type of guy?'

I seized the moment. 'I don't. So tell me about the guy you're with. What's he like?'

64

It was the wrong thing to say. Her eyes narrowed, her mood clouded. 'I don't want to talk about him,' she said. 'It's a nice afternoon, so don't spoil it.'

We were lying on beach towels, propped up on elbows, facing each other.

'I'd like to know,' I told her. 'You must know the effect you've had on me, even in just 48 hours.'

Nikki sat upright. She sprayed some sun-oil on her shoulders and turned her back to me, indicating I should rub the oil in. Could have been her shoulders were sore, could be she didn't want to face me.

'You caught me at a good time last night,' she said, gently rotating her head as I massaged the oil. The sensual texture of the hot skin rippled through my fingertips. 'I've been with Lee just over a year. He works at one of the clubs. You start off OK with someone but then you find they aren't who you thought they were. Something you said last night just reminded me of that. My heart doesn't beat faster when he's around. It never did.'

'Whatever the reason, thanks for coming today,' I said.

She turned around, leaned across and kissed me briefly on the cheek. There was a distinct heady smell of sun oil and perfume and I managed the supreme effort of not pulling her to me. We just held amused eye contact, neither of us speaking. Then a movement behind her distracted me. Coming towards us, fast and fixated, was a man displaying the same single-minded purpose as a charging rhino. He was tall and wide and stubble-headed, sweat glistening like splashed silver on his red contorted face. Big strides, boots sinking deep into the sand, and just ten metres away, close enough to see widened, bulging eyes and lips snarled back. He wore an army-style vest and combat trousers. It was clear he wasn't coming over to ask me to play frisbee.
Even before it registered that I'd seen that nasty snarl before - while I was pinned to the kitchen floor at my bungalow - I

65

knew it had to be Lee. My own expression must have signalled impending mayhem, for Nikki glanced over her shoulder and saw the rhino just as he was on us. 'Oh fuck,' she said, almost under her breath, scrambling aside and making herself a small target in the sand.

'Bitch. I thought I'd find you here.' He shouted so loud, it came out as a high-pitched scream and he kicked out at her crouched figure but she rolled clear and he didn't follow. He was heading for me, face set fierce like a tribal warrior. I tried to duck the punch but it caught me hard on the side of the jaw and I fell, but more off-balance than out. Lee came down on me knees first and I felt my ribs bending on impact. For a couple of seconds his raw toothy face was close up as he pinned down my shoulders with his knees, and then raised his fist. Unable to move, and insufficiently built to pitch him off, I waited for the pulped nose and smashed teeth.

Yet the punch never came. Something blurred across, sweeping him off me yelping and squealing as he rolled in the sand. There stood Nikki with a baseball bat held in both hands, the silver shaft splashed bright with blood. 'I knew this thing would come in useful one day,' she said, and threw it back into the Jeep. Lee was still sprawled on the ground, moaning quietly. The lower half of his face was at an adjusted angle and I thought his jaw was probably broken. Blood was gushing from his sliced cheek.

I looked at Nikki with amazed admiration. 'What now?' I asked.

She was calm and matter-of-fact and looked incredibly sexy, standing tall, shoulders back and breathing deeply. The effort of swinging the baseball bat had popped one breast out from her bikini top. She hadn't noticed and I wasn't telling.

'Are you hurt?' she said.

'I'm OK.'

She scooped up her bag and beach towels, and dumped them into the Jeep. Glancing down at Lee, who was still clutching at his face and whimpering, she said 'Let's go.'

'Where are we going?'

'Follow me in your car, OK?'

'OK. What about Lee?'

She looked at me scornfully. 'What he got, he deserved. If we hadn't split now it would have been soon. He'll live. Just follow me. I know a place we can go.'

I spun my car in a tight circle and tucked in behind the Jeep as it sped away. I didn't know where we were heading, or what would happen next. But then I seldom did.

Nikki turned south on the Pacific Coast Highway, back towards Santa Monica. Soon, on my left, I saw the cliffs of Pacific Palisades and its swanky movie star beach front homes. I'd heard Cruise, Hanks, Spielberg and other A-listers lived there, and one day I might ask Nikki to give me a tour. But not today. I was hurtling past at 60 miles an hour, fleeing from the wrath of a tough guy with a broken jaw and a score to settle. Nikki exited onto San Vincente, then turned off into a residential district, threading her way through bright white Spanish-style houses edged by lines of squat palm trees which stood like sentries along the street, their huge spiky shiny green fronds twitching lightly in the breeze. She parked the Jeep half on and half off the sidewalk, came over to me and said 'Wait here while I explain things to a friend. She'll help us.' I watched her walk up the short pathway and push the bell of a neat two-storey house with a dark green door flanked on one side by a massive creamy yucca and on the other by a thick stemmed man-high cactus. I could see Nikki having an animated conversation with a dark-haired girl. Then she turned and signalled me to come in.

'This is Estelle. She says we can stay here a few days. We should be OK. Lee doesn't know where she lives.'
I realised how little I knew about her life. 'I take it you and Lee live together?'

'Past tense,' she said. 'I'll pick up my stuff when he's out .'

'How come you got together with him? On short acquaintance, he doesn't seem a nice guy.'

'Usual story,' she said, shrugging. 'Didn't know what he was like when we first met and by the time you find out, you're kind of stuck with it.'

Estelle came back from the kitchen with an orange juice for Nikki and a cold bottle of Bud which she handed to me. 'From what I've heard, I guess you need a drink,' she said. She was right. I held the icy bottle for a few seconds against my aching jaw before taking long eager gulps.

Half an hour later Estelle showed us to our bedroom, a small square room at the back of the house with one tall shuttered window, and a small circular skylight, which sent down a huge slab of bright light onto white-sheeted double bed. I looked uncertainly at Nikki. Her eyes sparked with mischievous humour.

'You don't want your own room, do you?' she said, already knowing my answer.

That evening at about eight, soon after the sun had slid from sight leaving just a few stretched-out marker clouds of dull slate-grey, I set out to visit the home of Kirkland Ryan. I didn't know what I was trying achieve. It was a foolish plan and I knew it. The fact that Ryan had not only refused to see me but hadn't even bothered to ask why I was there was in itself suspicious. It suggested he either already knew, or didn't care. Both options told me I was onto something, though I didn't know what. I tried to reassure myself that when Marlowe reached an impasse, he tried to make something happen.

Earlier, I had opened up a little to Nikki about what I was doing, though she still knew nothing about the murders back in the UK. To her, I was still doing a background investigation on a fraud case. Even so, when I mentioned I was going to check out Ryan's house, she looked concerned. 'Be careful,' she said. 'You're not in England now. Here, we shoot first.'

I found Ryan's house easily enough, a couple of miles inland from Ventura, just off the road to Casitas Springs. It was a long, low crescent-shaped construction painted ivory white, and in front was a T-shaped swimming pool, the water a dark immobile oily-blue in the failing light. The villa was a lone building, a white daub in a stretch of dusty landscape, set well off the highway yet readily visible at a distance because of the flat terrain. Around the house was a high whitewashed wall some eight feet tall, broken only by an imposing arched entrance framing black iron gates. I stood at the gates like one of those hapless victims in a vampire movie. You always know that when they reach the entrance of the grim foreboding castle, seeking directions or reporting that their car has broken down, they are already doomed. Don't go in, you silently urge, but you know they will...

Although the scene in front of me was nothing like as fearsome as a turreted, fog-shrouded Transylvanian vampire lair, I did feel a sudden chill of anticipation. This was not a movie and not a game. Ryan was likely to be a dangerous man and I was set on confronting him, defying all logic and commonsense. All right, I wasn't planning to accuse him of murder, not there and then, to his face. I wanted merely to check him out, weigh him up, find out what my instinctive take was on this reclusive businessman who may have killed two people for a reason I didn't yet know. I was naive, and it was risky. But I had nothing else.

Set in the wall on the right-hand side of the tall arched gates was a white intercom box with a single red button. I decided to push the button.

A female voice spoke, quickly and briefly in Spanish. So I uttered one of the few Spanish phrases I knew. 'No comprendo Espanol.'

Silence for a few seconds, then in clipped English she said 'No one home.'

'When will someone be back?' I asked.

'No one home.'

End of conversation.

I drove back down the track about a quarter of a mile and parked the car off the road., I worked my way on foot across the rough ground towards the rear of the villa. At eight feet, the wall was high enough to be a deterrent to just hopping over, but not insurmountable. I gathered together two or three large boulders and stacked them so they gave me the lift I needed to get my hands on the top of the wall. The effort required reminded me that I needed more gym work.

I hauled myself up and over in one swift action, landing crouched down in the floral shrubbery I had seen from the gateway. Expensive landscaping had given the property a hotel-garden look, with strategically placed palms and a scattering of bushy plants tall enough to screen me. Though two ground-floor windows were showing lights, I could see no one about. It was then I remembered the picture of the Doberman on the gates. I should have remembered it before I got over the wall. Still, there was no sight or sound of dogs, so I decided to risk cutting thirty metres or so across open ground to a low flat-roofed extension at the rear. There were no dogs, no shouts of alarm, and so I edged along the wall and peeked in a window. I saw a large and luxurious kitchen. There was no one in sight. Without much difficulty I managed to scramble myself up onto the roof of the extension, using the window ledge and tenacious grip on the decorative stonework frieze, and keeping low, crept along until I could look in a first floor window.

It was a large rectangular room, equipped as an office. There were three desks and computers, but only one was occupied, by a girl with short-cut boyish hair and small square-framed spectacles who looked Japanese. Luckily, she was staring at a computer screen and not at the window. It could, I suppose, have been some legitimate business, yet I doubted it. I didn't know what Ryan was doing, or why, or if he was in any way connected with the death of an old woman in a wheelchair in a quiet Devon village thousands of miles away, but perhaps I was now a little closer to finding out.

The stark memory of Marjorie and the staring eyes of Krista Carlton reclining chic but dead in her sports car reinforced my feeling of total helplessness and frustration at my lack of deductive skills. I had no idea what I was doing, and even less about what I should be doing next. Retreating to consider the options seemed a wise choice. I made my way back across the roof and glancing over to make sure that there was no one about, I dropped neatly to the ground. Well, neatly was the intention but I landed awkwardly, losing my balance and toppling sideways like a clumsy kid. I pulled myself upright, flicking clinging grey dust from my shirt. It was then that I saw him staring at me and I recognised him immediately. After all, a Doberman is unmistakable.

6

There are times in your life when it essential to act before thinking, and if I'd had time to think about it, I'd have decided this was one of those times. But I didn't have time. I knew a lot about dogs. My family had always had dogs. But in the tenth of a second available I remembered only one thing. Dogs like to know who is in charge. If they don't know, then they think they are.

I straightened up to full height, took a brisk step forward and snapped 'Sit!'

The dog hesitated for a moment and I repeated the word again, voice sharp as a whip. The dog sat. I now had a second or two to reason, and I thought it likely that a guard dog would have been trained to a few relatively simple commands. So it probably knew 'stay'.

I made eye contact with the dog, and snapped out the phrase with the full authority of a German Commandant. I started to walk towards the perimeter wall. I didn't look back, and I didn't run. At any moment I expected to hear the scrape of claws on the hard surface but it didn't happen. I shinned up a tree to hoist myself back on the top of the wall and it was only then that I turned round and looked. forty metres away close to the house, the tall black dog sat like an Egyptian statue. Dogs can be wonderful, obedient creatures.

I jogged back to my car, hot and dusty and with a tear in the knee of my jeans. They were new only last week. Funny how little things irritate you. Driving back, I decided another visit to Ryan's villa was required, but at a time when no one was at home. I would have to stake it out and keep watch. After bouncing the dusty Chrysler up onto the sidewalk outside Estelle's house, I walked in, hot and weary and aching, and found Nikki was there, looking fresh and pretty. She was wearing a short lime-green wrap-around skirt and a tight white off-the-shoulder top, borrowed from Estelle, I assumed. Smiling, fussing around me, questioning me about the trip, she handed me a large glass of red wine, and pointed me in the direction of the shower. 'Don't be long,' she said firmly. 'We'll be eating in about 20 minutes.'

I was humbled by the perfection of it all.

A couple of hours later, we were locked together in the big double bed, the room lit only by candles. Above us was the soft rhythmic swish of the large ceiling fan. She had undressed slowly at the bottom of the bed, then came sliding over me like a large smooth warm snake, moving upwards, slow and purposeful until she pressed her breasts lightly against my scarred and scuffed face, whispering 'There, does that feel better now?'

I took it to be a rhetorical question.

Noon next day saw me arriving at the Lahoya restaurant, just a few minutes drive from Estelle's house at Marina Del Rey, a man-made harbour south of Santa Monica centre. I was there to meet a Mexican dancer called Mahita.

You expect a dancer to be tall, and she was, about five feet ten and most of that was her legs. The rest of her measured up pretty well too, but though she had long dark hair and hot sultry eyes, she had a sullen face, the corners of her mouth slightly turned down. There was also a slight thickening of flesh around the jaw line and neck, suggesting she may not have her head-turning looks for too many years longer. In a way, that was the reason I was meeting her. She had recently been dumped for a younger woman, and very significantly, the man who had dumped her was none other than Kirkland Ryan.

'She's mad as hell about it,' Boyd had told me that morning when he called me. His network of contacts had finally produced some sort of lead. Through a friend of a friend of a friend he'd got to Mahita. He had suggested to her I was willing to pay for information, and she proved willing to meet for a discussion, mainly I suspected about how much I might pay. I don't know whether she needed the money or needed revenge, but she had been ready enough to meet up, with Boyd there too in the potential role of negotiator. By now, I'd had to fill him in on the true background of the case.

The restaurant was one of many crowding Mindinao Way. It was a pretty place with lots of tubbed shrubs and flowers around an imposing arch of steel and bronzed glass. Boyd and Mahita were already there at one of the outside tables when I arrived, being served drinks by a stick-thin waiter who looked like an emaciated Walter Matthau.

'I ordered you a beer,' called Boyd as I strode up. 'This is Mahita.'

She looked up at me in brief acknowledgement, unsmiling and appearing disinterested, then continued to use a straw to play with the ice cubes in her mineral water. Perhaps she felt that playing hard to get would enable her to boost her asking price. I said nothing, just studied her. She was wearing a long-sleeved crimson shirt, open at the neck, tight black trousers and black boots with a high Cuban heel. Her finger-nails were longer than the claws on a long-clawed eagle and they tapped impatiently on the frosted glass top of the table.

Still I said nothing. I just eyed her carefully. No doubt about it, she was a still terrific looker who exuded a seismic sexual frisson. When in her early twenties, she would have created havoc among the male population. But she wasn't in her early twenties now. She was mid-thirties at a guess, maybe a couple of years more, and she had the acid profile that always hallmarks a woman who has been discarded for a younger version. She was sulky and resentful, smouldering quietly and dangerously, just waiting for a spark. My feigned lack of interest set off her short fuse and she exploded into a torrent of demands and abuse.

In essence, it amounted to this: she was prepared to talk

about Ryan, but she wanted $5,000 up front. It seemed to me she was demanding a lot for what might turn out to be a little. Before I could speak, Boyd took his cue and started to negotiate. After some initial resistance, she settled for $2,000 to start off, with the promise of more if the information was significant. She began at warp-speed, gesticulating and tossing her head and flicking her hair, her tone a roller-coaster of pitch and emotion. It was five minutes before she drew breath.

Mahita confirmed Ryan's business was a scam. 'Every month he invoices tens of thousands of companies all over Europe by post and by email for entries in business directories that are never published,' she said. The invoices were for small amounts usually just below $100, and a surprisingly high number were paid automatically because in the scale of corporate accounting, amounts under $100 were insignificant and there was no need to seek payment approval from higher up the chain. Mostly, nobody made any checks. Done on a grand scale, over many countries, the operation netted Ryan millions a year. And every year he changed the titles of his companies and the directories and did the whole thing all over again. He lived in America to distance himself from the scam and to some extent from European jurisdiction. Extradition for fraud was expensive and time-consuming and was way down the priority list. It was encouraging to have it confirmed that Ryan was not a legitimate businessman, merely a con-man, but it still didn't tie in. 'Does Ryan collect paintings,' I asked, trying to make a connection between him and Marjorie.

Mahita said he didn't, which wasn't what I wanted to hear. She started another tirade of abuse, bad-mouthing Ryan. There was so much venom in her voice, it could have etched a pattern on her glass.

Boyd and I spent another ten or fifteen minutes firing questions at the smouldering dancer, trying to find some even remote possibility to pursue, some hopeless longshot that an out-of-ideas detective could clutch at and perhaps nurture. Sometimes, fate can come up with a lucky break, a pointer in the right direction just when you need it most. But not today.

All that was left to do was to question Mahita about Ryan's movements and the security systems at his house. She said he went to his Ivar Avenue office most days, seldom went out in the evenings, and rarely had visitors. He mainly used a black Mercedes when he did go out. He had one trusted assistant, a man called Leon and two Japanese girls who worked at his house. Leon was resident, but the other staff were locals who didn't live in, and usually finished around 4 pm. Then there was Ryan's new girlfriend. She didn't live at the villa but she often stayed over, mainly weekends. She was blonde Texan, 20 years old and her name was Alicia.

'Cheap hooker!' added Mahita, banging the table with a clenched fist.

And that was it. Mahita left clutching $2,000, still murmuring expletives, gravel spraying high and wide as her red Honda left the car park at racing pace.

Boyd asked me the question I hoped he wasn't going to ask. 'What next?'

'How should I know,' I said, rather bitterly 'I'm just letting this thing run on its own. I just jump out of the way now and then.'

'Take some advice,' said Boyd. 'Let it go. Ryan seems a dangerous guy to take on. If you're sensible, you'll take your pretty new girlfriend back to England. Life is too short.'

'It was short for Krista Carlton,' I said. 'I owe it to her to carry on. Even though she knew I was a loser, she put her trust in me. And anyone who saw old Marjorie gunned down as she sat blind and helpless in the wheelchair would want to carry on. I just wish I had a game-plan. I'm stumbling in the dark.'

Boyd shrugged sympathetically and got up. 'I'm glad it's not my problem. Good luck, my friend.'

I watched his car disappear between the lines of nodding palms, the high sun giving the big, droopy fronds a silver sheen. I sat pondering, peeling thin, damp strips from the label on my beer bottle. Then I remembered Marlowe's maxim: when nothing happens, make a phone call.

Nikki answered almost right away. 'How did it go?' she asked immediately. It boosted me that she seemed so pleased to hear from me. My self-confidence was so low, it was somewhere under my shoes.

'It went OK, lots of information but no leads.'

Then I heard myself telling her I was going back up to Ryan's house to attempt to see him. It was news to me. I couldn't remember deciding on that.

'Just take care,' said Nikki. 'No going in like Rambo, OK?'

'Don't worry. There's no way Max Slater and Rambo can fit in the same sentence. They're a contradiction in terms.'

'I love the way you'll use fifty words when you could have used five,' she said. 'Just be careful.'

I told her I would be back at Estelle's before dark.

I headed straight up to Ryan's walled fortress and this time, I planned to try the direct approach, parking right outside the tall wrought-iron gates. I was about to ring the bell when I saw movement at the top of the long driveway. Someone was washing a black Mercedes. It took a minute or so of shouting to attract his attention but then he slowly walked towards me, his pace arrogantly languid. I guess he was in his mid-twenties, dark hair, good looking but with a distinctly unfriendly manner. His eyes were narrow slits as he faced me through the bars. He said nothing, just looked tough and waited for me to speak. I explained it was important I saw Mr Ryan. It was very urgent.

The valet squeezed out the sponge that he carried down with him as if he was wringing my neck. His mouth moved into a smirk he'd probably seen in an Antonio Banderas movie. 'Mr

Ryan is busy. No visitors.' He turned his back and started to walk away.

'Hey!' I shouted, but he ignored me and went back to washing the Mercedes. I saw no point in trying the bell or intercom again, so I pointedly drove away. My irritation level was soaring. I was furious at the dismissive refusal and furious with myself for being so inept. Looping the Chrysler, I headed back. About two miles down the road I was still angry - I had given up too easily. I turned around and again drove towards the villa, no plan in mind except to be more persistent and see what happened.

When the villa came into sight, I got the break I felt was long overdue. As I approached the gates, they swung open to allow out a small car, probably one of the staff had finished their shift. I made a sweeping half-turn across the road and was inside the gates before they began to close. I drove fast up the driveway and stopped just short of the front entrance to the villa. The car-washer I had seen earlier threw done his wash-leather and came towards me. Then there was a shout from the house, and he stopped, backing away. In the entrance was a tall man dressed in black and he was heading my way with a purposeful stride and a tight-set face. A few yards from my car, he paused. Then I noticed it. Clenched tight in his right hand was something round and dark and before I could really focus, he tossed it through the open window of the Chrysler. The black silhouette of the grenade blurred past my face long before my stunned brain sent an SOS signal to my limbs, and I heard a soft thud as it landed.

I shouldered open the car door and fell out, my shoulder slamming hard onto driveway. It was a single fluent move borne of panic and I lay face down awaiting a shattering explosion. But there was no explosion, no searing pain, no metal slivers dicing me to prime mince-meat. All I heard was laughter. The man in black and the hired help were laughing uncontrollably, high-fiving each other. I lifted my head, bewildered and feeling foolish.

'You scare easily,' said Ryan, smoothing back his hair and

showing perfect white teeth in a wide, mocking grin. He stepped past me, reached into the car and showed me the grenade It wasn't black and it wasn't metal. It was a dark purple and he bit into it with his neat even teeth. It was a peach.

I felt as small and crushed as I did at fourteen when a girl I worshipped rejected my stumble-tongued advance.

'Forgive my little joke,' said Ryan, reaching down to help me up. 'I thought you might appreciate something theatrical after your dramatic entrance.'

I scrambled to my feet, ignoring his outstretched hand, and began dusting down my clothes. I hadn't got a witty response so I stayed silent.

'Come inside,' he said, turning towards the villa. 'I'll be interested to hear what you want, and why you felt the need to come here uninvited.' His voice was relaxed, unconcerned. Here was man who felt he was in total control.

We walked into a large circular lobby, about the size of the foyer of a small hotel. The floor was faded terracotta tiles, and from the centre rose a wide cedar-wood staircase. Stark against the white walls were various shoulder-high shrubs in dark green cube pots. Ryan walked to the right and opened a pair of double doors into a large living room. Although it was bright with the low sun still streaming in, it had the dead-air smell of a room rarely used. There were no tangible signs of human occupation, no personal touches. There were two beige leather sofas and four matching armchairs, evenly distributed around the rectangular room. There was a centre table of dark smoked glass with a wrought iron frame, surrounded by six high-backed bronze-finish metal chairs. There were no pictures on the walls, no ornaments, bowls of fruit or flowers, no magazines or books. It was a big white room which to me exuded a still and silent sense of foreboding.

Ryan sat down in one of the armchairs and waved for me to be seated opposite. He was slim and fit and looked well-manicured. His thick black hair had recently been cut, and it had a mellow gleam of gel. His black trousers looked new, his black shirt hung well enough to have been hand-made. He wore no jewellery, and the only items that caught the eye were a silver buckle on his black leather belt, and a black-faced watch on his left wrist.

'Start by introducing yourself and explaining why you are here,' he said.

'My name is Max Slater. I'm a private detective from England. 'I've made several attempts to contact you, all without success. I suppose my frustration got the better of me.'

'I retired here for solitude and tranquillity,' he said. 'I don't like uninvited visitors and the staff have been instructed to discourage them.'

I went in with a hard point to try to jolt him. 'You've made several attempts to buy a painting from a family called Carlton, back in England. I'd like to know why.'

Ryan didn't twitch in his chair, his face didn't flush, his eyes didn't blink. The only visual clue was there were no visual clues and I thought there should have been.

'Why should that be any concern of yours?' he said, as if merely making conversation.

'I represent the family.'

'So they wish to sell?'

'Possibly,' I stalled. 'But they are puzzled why you are so keen to pay a high price for a painting that has no significance. The painter was a nobody.'

'Collecting is such a strange obsession,' said Ryan. 'Who can say why certain things attract us? I just feel Stackford is very under-rated.'

I pulled together a few shreds from my distant A-level art days. 'I suppose you think that because he was once a pupil of Thomas Gainsborough, his work might well rise in value?'

'Exactly. It may take a few years but its worth a gamble. That's part of the fascination of collecting art.'

That response was significant. Stackford could not have been Gainsborough's pupil, they lived more than 100 years apart. Ryan was obviously no art-collector, so he was lying about his interest in the painting. At last I'd actually done what detectives are supposed to do. I had found a clue.

'Two members of the Carlton family have been killed in the past year.'

Ryan looked surprised. 'That's terrible! Car accident?'

'They were murdered.'

In fairness, Ryan did seem shocked, but the expression flicked on and off as if he had just pressed a switch. 'I'm sorry to hear that,' he said. 'But then England is such a dangerous place these days.'

He got up and took two or three steps towards me. 'Let's get right to the point, Mr Slater. What exactly is it you want from me?'

There was no obvious answer to that. This was meant to be just a reconnaissance mission. I could hardly accuse him of the murders. There was no evidence at all, just my vague suspicions.

'You've told me all I need to know,' I said, also standing up. 'I'll tell the family your interest is genuine and perhaps they'll be in touch.'

It was a deeply unconvincing story, and I wished I had a better exit line. Ryan was looking at me rather pensively. 'I'll give some thought to increasing my offer for the painting,' he said. 'Where can I reach you?'

If I tried to avoid answering, it could make him more suspicious than he already was. It would have been easy to lie, give the name of a hotel, but that could easily be checked out so I gave him the address of Terry's bungalow. It didn't matter because it I wasn't staying there now, and Terry was still in England. I was aware that there might be another attempt on my life – Ryan or someone he had hired had tried to make me a hit-and-run victim at the airport the day I arrived. I'd just have to stay much more alert than I had been so far.

As I stood up to leave, I intentionally knocked a cushion onto the floor and stooped to retrieve it. That gave me the opportunity to take a closer look at Ryan's shoes because a tiny glint had caught my eye while I sat facing him. That split-second glance was all I needed to see that the tiny gleam on the side of Ryan's shoes was a little gold motif. It was in the shape of a rodeo rider and the last time I had seen identical shoes, they were on the feet of a man burgling my office in Exeter.

7

At around 6am, the bright white light of the sun started to slant in around the bedroom curtains, fanning out across the walls. Outside, the cloudless sky would be a hard translucent blue and the ground temperature still cool. There were faint sounds of early morning activity, a car starting, a distant shout, but none of them had wakened me. I had been awake for several hours, too much turning over endlessly in my mind. Nikki was lying asleep at my side, breathing almost inaudibly, one arm draped across my stomach.

I couldn't get my thoughts away from the meeting with Ryan, the uneasy, threatening feeling it had instilled in me. His perfunctory goodbye had been too matter of fact, too unconcerned and I was unsettled as I drove back to Estelle's.

When I arrived, Estelle was out, staying overnight with a relative down the coast at Inglewood. I told Nikki I'd met Ryan, but that the meeting was inconclusive. I didn't go into detail. After eating, we spent the rest of the evening curled up on the sofa, drinking chilled Napa Valley wine and talking, exhanging life stories, likes and dislikes, and eventually she started asking more about my work. Despite my reservations and probably too much wine, I decided to take a chance on filling her in on some of the background, including the two murders.

Far from being unnerved, she seemed excited. 'It's just like a private eye movie,' she said. 'Have you seen The Big Sleep?'

'You've heard of Philip Marlowe? I'm amazed someone of your age would know who he was!'

She punched my shoulder in mock-anger. 'I did modern American literature at college,' she said reprovingly.

'Raymond Chandler, Dashiell Hammett, all of them. Chandler was my favourite, I loved Marlowe, he was so cool.'

'At least Marlowe usually knew what he was doing,' I said. 'He always had an instinct about what the case was about, while I just stumble around without being able to see the big picture. I'm convinced that Ryan killed Marjorie and Krista, but I've no idea why and I certainly can't go to the police. All I've got is suspicions, and absolutely no evidence. And Ryan's a local resident and businessman. Chances of the police taking me seriously are remote.'

'How come you became a detective if you say you're no good at it?' said Nikki, shifting so she lay on my chest, face just inches from mine.

'Too many movies like the The Big Sleep, I suppose. Those 1940s detectives had a certain shabby glamour – and they usually got the girl in the end.'

'You're doing better than you think,' Nikki said, inching forward and kissing me full on the lips. 'You've got the girl at the beginning!'

'That's what bothers me,' I said, getting serious for a moment. 'Why me? I'm a lot older than you, and I don't look like Johnny Depp either.'

She kissed me again. 'Guys my age are a waste of space. It's all baseball and getting drunk. They treat you like shit. I knew that's how it would be with Lee. I don't know why I bothered. My mother always told me to look for an older man.'

'You should always listen to your mother,' I said, pulling her onto me.

Later, with Nikki asleep, I lay still with just the low hum of the ceiling fan breaking the silence. My mind was magnetically focussed on Ryan. My judgement was that he was a cold empty man who concentrated on his own life to the exclusion of everyone else's. Alone in his clinical home

– you couldn't count hired help as friends – he exuded a rather spooky creepiness. Yet whenever I thought of the man, whatever my judgement of his character, it didn't help me get any nearer learning why he wanted a worthless old painting so much he would kill to get it. I could see only a couple of options.

One was that for some reason I couldn't fathom, the painting was potentially of huge value, and it would have to be huge because Ryan was already a rich man. I didn't like that option because it would mean a respected art dealer like Jeremy Le Roye was wrong, and so too was the valuer the family had called in a couple of years earlier. There was no mystery about the artist, he was in the reference books, he had a track record. But his paintings were worth very little, a few hundred pounds at best. They could not suddenly be worth millions.

The other option was that the killings were a way of sending an unmistakable message to the Carlton family. That message was for them to give up the painting. Two had refused, and those two were now dead. So what could it be about the painting that was so important?

I was no nearer coming up with an answer when the sun rose.

It was about 11am when Estelle came back. We were out on the rear patio just lounging and chatting. Estelle came out to see us, excited over a news flash on the car radio. There had been a shooting at a house in Santa Monica. A man was dead.

' Where did this happen?' I asked.

'East side, I think they said Pico Street.'
I needed to know the exact address. My bungalow was on Pico Street and I had a unnerving feeling that I might have been the target. But I was here and very much alive, so who was the dead man?

Estelle had barely finished speaking before I was on the phone to Boyd. I cut short his small talk, explained what had happened, and asked him if he could use his Press status to get anymore information about the incident, particularly the victim. He promised to get back to me as soon as he got any details. As I put down the phone, I noticed my hand was shaking. The incident was disturbing, a sudden reminder of my vulnerability. I'd been trying to keep the danger at the back of my mind, not just because it might scare Nikki but because in truth, I didn't want to acknowledge it myself. I was now convinced that Ryan had plans for me. It wasn't the right time or place when I was at his house, but I had an uneasy feeling he would try to find the right time and place.

At the moment, Ryan didn't know where I was staying, but I couldn't be sure how long that situation might last. Santa Monica was a relatively small place, word might be out among Ryan's contacts. I just had to make progress on the case. I didn't have time to let it unfold at its own pace, if it ever would. It was essential I became more pro-active, forced the situation. I was still edging around the subject when about 20 minutes later Boyd rang back. What he told me confirmed my first instinct - it was my bungalow on Pico Street where the shooting had occurred.

'The victim was shot twice in the head from behind, happened about midnight. He was on the driveway. The body wasn't found until this morning. LA's finest are still making neighbourhood enquiries.'

Then Boyd told me something that sent shock rippling.

'This is unofficial, from a police contact,' he said, lowering his voice. 'It's not on the news yet. The man who was killed had ID in the name of Lee Brooks. You know him?'

I knew him. Lee Brooks was Nikki's ex-boyfriend. He must have gone back to the bungalow to settle his score with me. In the darkness he must have been mistaken for me returning home. Suddenly, I didn't like playing detective. And playing was the word. There was no glamour now, just another body, and the chilling knowledge that I was probably next in line.

There was no point in delaying. Though I didn't want to do

it, I knew I had to break the news to Nikki. I called her in from her sunbed, sat her down, knelt in front of her and placed my hands on her shoulders. She knew something was seriously wrong before I spoke, her eyes wide and wondering. As quickly as I could, I told her the shooting was at the bungalow where I had been staying, that a man had been killed, and that man was Lee. He was probably mistaken for me. She took it quite well. By that, I mean she cried only for about half an hour, clinging to me like a child. I let her cry herself out. Eventually, she spoke between sobs, gulping the air. 'I didn't like him, and a couple of times when we had a fight, I said I'd kill him,' she said. 'But I didn't really want him dead.'

'Neither did I, but somebody did,' I said. 'It was meant to be me, and the only suspect is Ryan. I've stepped too close to whatever he's up to, and now I'm a target.'

We looked at each other helplessly, a short silence dragging by.

'There's still no point in going to the police,' I said. 'There would be too many questions and I don't have the answers. I might even be arrested as suspect. The house is unoccupied, the owner is over in the UK. I'll give Terry a call, tell him I moved out a few days ago and that I've heard on the news a man has been shot dead in the driveway. I'll say I know nothing about it, but if he gets a call from the LA police, would he keep my name out of it anyway. He will. We go back a long way.'

Nikki was just staring blankly. I don't think she had taken in a word I'd said. 'Don't worry', I told her. 'I want us out of this. I just need some evidence that ties in Ryan. Once I've got that, I'll go to the police, I promise.'

She was still slumped on the chair, nervously twisting strands of her hair. Putting my arms around her, I drew her to me.

'Why don't we just take off?' she asked suddenly. 'We could go stay with my mom in Salinas. Or you could take me to London.'

89

I shook my head. 'I'd always be looking over my shoulder. After all, he knew exactly when I arrived here. Either he or somebody else tried to run me down. He knew I was on the case after burgling my office. He probably had the airport watched. There was a picture of me in the UK Press, so he knew what I looked like. And I'll bet the only reason he let me leave last night was because he didn't want my death or disappearance connected with his house. I could have told someone where I was going. Sure, we can probably get out of town, but I don't think we could ever feel safe. Ryan has already had three people killed, two of them back in England. If he can kill at that distance, nowhere is safe. If would be just a matter of time.'

My mobile rang and it was Boyd again. 'Interesting development,' he said. 'I've had a phone call from Mahita. She wants another meeting and more money. But this time, she says she's going to tell us the whole truth.'

'Could be a try on, just squeezing us for more cash.'

'Maybe. But she seems scared and she wants to leave town. She says if you will pay her off, she'll tell us want we really want to know.'

'And what's that?' I wasn't sure I knew myself any more.

'She says she'll tell us about a painting Ryan was trying to acquire from England.'

8

Next day was bright and clear with the temperature climbing and a strong sun pressing hard on the paving on Estelle's patio. A light feathery breeze was snuffling around the place with a pleasant cool touch, but I wasn't relaxing and improving my tan. I was wearing a T-shirt and Chinos and sitting in the shade of a large striped umbrella, fretful and impatient.

Close by, Nikki lay face down taking the full heat of the sun, wearing just a bikini bottom, and with a bright red baseball cap shading her head. Her arms hung languidly over the sides of the lounger. At breakfast she had been a little subdued, but she seemed to have come to terms with the death of Lee. I don't think she had much feeling left for him anyway. I guess I'd come along at just the right time for her. Now, she was concerned about me, and had become noticeably more clingy. Every thirty minutes, she would ask me to promise I wouldn't do anything foolish or dangerous. That was the kind of promise I could give easily. I just lied.

In another hour, it would be time to leave for a meeting with Boyd and Mahita. It kept nagging at me that this might be some kind of set-up, and that she may still be in contact with Ryan, or was being used as a lure. Of course, I'd voiced this view to Boyd but he dismissed it, convinced Mahita was on the level, and I kept telling myself I should trust his instinct. He'd spent quite a long time on the phone cajoling her into further co-operation. It was certain too that he was an excellent judge of character – journalists usually are. They've heard everything hundreds of times and have learned to recognise smokescreens, identify accomplished liars and spot hidden agendas.

Boyd said that at the first meeting, Mahita was testing us out, perhaps to ascertain just how much money we might be good for, and partly perhaps to ensure we weren't working for Ryan. She was clearly very frightened of him. One thing was certain, however. She urgently needed cash. After falling out with Ryan, who had kept her, she had no means of support. Too old to cut it as a dancer, until she could find a new guy she was broke. 'Right now, she says wants to go home to Momma,' said Boyd.

Momma was in Tijuana, and Mahita needed money to get there, plus more to tide her over until, presumably, she could find another man to keep her. It wouldn't take her that long. She still had the body and that hot, sensual look going for her, at least for another couple of years.

In conversation with Boyd, she had asked for $5,000, but it might be negotiable, especially if she was desperate. I smiled thinly at the thought. It was me who was desperate. In truth, it was hurting me that I hadn't made any progress, hadn't come up with one significant scrap of information since the case had started. I was an amateur and it was showing. Boyd probably knew it, and it wouldn't be long before Nikki reached the same conclusion. My despondency had an acid, bitter edge to it, and I leaned back in my chair, devoid of any positive thoughts. My detective hero Philip Marlowe rarely found himself in such circumstances, but when he was disappointed with his efforts, I recalled him saying he would just sit around 'disadmiring myself.'

I started to practice.

The sun climbed higher and became more ruthless, burning my shoulder through my shirt as it cut away the shade from the big parasol. Another perfect day in a semi-tropical paradise and I had to waste it following what was likely to be a false trail instead of massaging oil into Nikki's taut young flesh.

Glancing across at her, she seemed to be asleep but her feet were gently tapping the air to the music from her iPhone. She looked so sweet, so innocent. What the hell was I doing? Why had I dragged her into this? My self-loathing was sliding out of control when suddenly, somehow sensing I was there,

Nikki flipped over to face me, pushing back her cap and then sitting upright. I watched her breasts gently settle. Beneath the broad peak of the red cap, her silver-grey eyes were honest and trusting. She reached out, squeezing my hand, and whispered 'Take care.'

'OK,' I said. 'Got to go now.' I stooped to kiss her, then left without looking back.

The meeting had been set up at a beachfront café at Venice, just a five-minute drive for me. I parked the car and walked to the rendezvous, weaving through the stream of joggers, cyclists and bikini-clad roller-bladers toning their tans and muscles, and side-stepping a small crowd watching a paunchy, balding guy jumping off a stool onto broken glass.

The long boardwalk promenade was fringed by restaurants, cafes and bars, tables bulging out onto the walkway and waiters darting among the passers-by with trays precariously balanced. Today, as on most days, Venice beach had a nice, friendly feel to it, and as the sun scattered random diamond flashes onto the lazy shifting turquoise sea and children chased each other along the bright white sand, it was hard to believe that my business in this resort arose directly from brutal deaths.

Light was bouncing off the pale-washed walls of the low buildings, causing me to squint behind my sun-glasses. Ahead I could see my destination, a seafood restaurant called Marinero, it's blue and yellow striped awning shading the sidewalk tables from the midday solar blowtorch.

Boyd and Mahita were already there, seated at a table right at the edge. Boyd waved, Mahita acknowledged me with an almost imperceptible nod of the head. She had her usual moody expression. She was wearing tight white jeans with diamond segments cut out from hip to ankle down both sides, her natural tan showing teasingly through. Her white bolero-type top left her arms, shoulders and navel bare. She was wearing a total of eight rings and five bracelets. She was the kind of girl that men, including Ryan, rewarded well for fulfilling their dark fantasies.

I sat opposite her. It was time to get tough. Taking out a thick bundle of crisp new bank notes, with deliberate slowness I counted out $2,500 and pushed the stack towards her. The other half I placed in front of me and covered them with my hand. I looked at Mahita. 'Start talking. Tell us everything you know and if I'm satisfied I have all the answers, you get the rest of the money.'

Boyd looked impressed. Mahita snatched up the cash and started talking. She spoke for maybe five minutes, with me slotting in occasional questions. Her manner seemed less truculent and more open than it had at the first meeting. She said Ryan had a room at his house which he normally always kept locked. One day a few months ago when Mahita was staying there, she noticed the door of this room was ajar, and thinking Ryan was there, went in. But he wasn't in, he'd gone downstairs to give instructions to his driver.

'What was in there?' I was leaning forward, anxious.

'A picture gallery.'

'I knew it! I knew he collected paintings. Now we're getting somewhere.'

'I think not, amigo,' said Mahita, shaking her head. 'There were no paintings in the room, just framed photographs.'

'Photographs? Of what?'

'People.'

'What kind of people?'

'All kinds. Old, young, even children. Old photos, black and white.'

'And that's it? Where the hell does that leave us?'
Mahita shrugged. 'I don't know. It is for you to make sense

of it, not me.'

'That's not enough for the money,' I said irritably. ' I need more.'

Mahita gave me a venomous look. Her voice rose half an octave as she spoke, hands gesticulating as if she was juggling. She called me a name in Mexican and though I didn't speak the language, the tone told me it was an obscenity.

'You are trying to cheat me,' she spat. 'All men are cheats.'

'I must be missing something here,' I snapped. 'When we set up this meeting you said you'd tell us about the painting, remember? Why is it so important?'

'I don't know. One day I heard Ryan talking to Leon about a painting he needed for this special room. He said a trip to England would be necessary.'

'Why the hell didn't you tell me that before!'

'You didn't give me the chance.'

'This time, I think she's told the truth,' Boyd ventured.

He was probably right, but I wasn't ready to let Mahita go yet. 'She could be making it all up for the money, telling us what she feels we want to hear?' I said, wanting her to hear the remark.

Mahita glared. Boyd spread his hands wide. 'I think it is the truth, but who knows?' he said.

My hopes of a big breakthrough had crashed. OK, this appeared to confirm Ryan wanted the painting, and that he had intended to get it. And it confirmed he had been to England. But it didn't explain why he wanted it, and until I knew that, I was still stuck.

Mahita started gabbling again. 'I have told you everything,' she said, holding out her hand for the rest of the money. 'There is no reason for me to lie. Since I hurt Ryan, I don't feel safe.'

'Hurt him? How?'

Mahita smiled at the memory. 'Two weeks ago we had big fight. I smash a wine-glass into his face. His cheek was cut open, big cut, many stitches at the hospital. That was when I left him.'

I suddenly felt very, very cold, the shiver quite violent as if there was ice on my spine.

The Ryan I had met just two days ago didn't have any scars on his face.

9

Stupid. Stupid. Stupid. Stupid. Stupid.

Late afternoon, almost early evening. The sun still blazed but it had lost much of its power as it headed for its horizon exit, and the low hills off to the west were hazing into a soft-edged deep blue. Across the terrace of Estelle's garden, long shadows were beginning to inch towards me.

Stupid. How could I have been so stupid?

I had been slumped in a lounger for at least two hours, reflecting bitterly on the comedic end to my meeting with Mahita. Several empty Bud bottles stood on the floor by my side. Nikki had eventually become bored with my introspection and had gone inside to chat with Estelle. Now and then, she would bring out a fresh beer for me, pointedly put it down, and walk away.

Stupid, fundamental error.

The first thing they do when they train you as a journalist is tell you never to make assumptions. And what had I done? I had assumed the man in black who met me at Ryan's villa was Ryan. He didn't actually say he was, and now, when I came to think of it, I hadn't asked. When I had described the man in black who met me at Ryan's house, Mahita started laughing. She told me the man I had met was Leon, a long-time friend of Ryan's who was employed to fix the kind of things Ryan himself couldn't or wouldn't do. Like killing people.

My clumsy mistake had jolted me, but at least had the dividend of harnessing my attention. Though feeling foolish and embarrassed, I found myself surprisingly re-energised, my blood tingling and my mind racing. Anxious to capitalise on this new information, I had started rapidly questioning Mahita.

She didn't know that much about Leon, but enough for it all to begin to fit in. According to her account, he and Ryan had come to California together three years ago, bought a house and set up their directory scam, fronted by an LA office to give the appearance of legitimacy. From there, a small number of directories were actually published. But they had worked the scheme for years across Europe, sending out tens of thousands of fake invoices every month, always for small amounts below $100 which were usually paid without any checking by accounts departments.

It seemed Leon was ex-army and had gone freelance for a while in the Balkans. He and Ryan had met in the Czech Republic, when Ryan hired him through an intermediary to take care of two local men who were also operating a fake-invoice racket in Prague. They were pulled out of the Vltava river a few days later but they hadn't drowned. Not unless water had seeped in through the bullet holes in the back of their heads.

It wasn't clear – and Mahita didn't know - whether Ryan and Leon were business partners, or Leon just a trusted hired hand. Either way it didn't matter, because Leon was the Mr Fix It and I was now on his list.

After Mahita had told all she knew, or maybe all she intended to tell, I paid her off. Boyd and I ordered fresh beers and watched her walk away. She was one of those women you just had to watch. 'There goes a lot of trouble for some man,' I said. 'I'm glad it's not me.'

Boyd smiled. 'I think I could handle her,' he said.

'Yeah?'

'Well, at least for a couple of nights!'

We laughed, but only for a moment. The cold uneasy,

reality of the situation was ever-present, and Boyd was urging caution.

'These seem real bad guys,' he said, placing a hand on my arm. 'My advice is to go to the cops. I'll help you. They'll listen to me.'

'It all comes down to evidence,' I said. 'And there is none. Even if the police go to Ryan's house, all they may find is evidence of fraud. I want them nailed for murder.'

'You may be the next victim,' said Boyd. 'Leon is clever. He didn't kill you when you paid him a visit because he knew you would have told someone where you were going. You never shit in your own bed.'

He was right, of course. Leon was just biding his time. The smart move would be to leave town. But this was now very personal. I was incensed at the casual ease of the killing of Marjorie, Krista and now Lee, incensed at how lightly Ryan viewed murder, how lightly he would dispose of me and perhaps Nikki too. All I knew right now was that I had to see this through without police help, at least at this stage. I couldn't run from it. It was another foolish, futile decision, I knew that. I tried to justify it by resolving to get out when I judged the time was right. I just knew that time wasn't now.

When I had arrived back at Estelle's, Nikki could tell something was wrong when she saw my tight-set face, and she too had laughed when I lamely explained how I had met the wrong man. My shame was profound. Now, as the skyline began to turn pale platinum, a frisky breeze danced in, quickly cooling the air. A few dry leaves began to rustle around the patio and I started to feel chilled. I went inside, opened a bottle of red wine, and slumped onto the sofa. My intention was to try to concoct a new plan, one which would inevitably involve getting into Ryan's villa again, more specifically getting into that special room. Surely it had to contain some sort of evidence to tie him to the Carlton murders? My luck must be due to turn. If I could just get even a sliver of hard evidence, I'd take my chances with the police.

Nikki had showered and came down to see me, looking cool and fresh and endlessly touchable in a white dressing gown which was just as short as a mini-skirt. I pulled her down onto my lap and told her I wanted to kiss every square inch of her.

'And just which particular square inch would you like to start with?' she asked. I should have taken the offer but instead I broke it to her that I needed to go back up to Ryan's place.

'You'll get caught,' she said. 'You've been lucky to get out both times you've been there.'

'It can be done,' I insisted. 'All I need is a plan.'

'Do you like Matt Damon?' she asked suddenly.

'I've seen a few of his movies, why?'

'Do you remember the one where he needed to break into a house to get some evidence, but it was heavily guarded?'

'No.'

'Maybe it wasn't him, but whoever it was, he set up a diversion. He got them all out of the place on a wild goose chase, and then while they were out, in he went.'

'Simple as that,' I said.

'Yes,' she said sharply. My rather dismissive tone had stung her.

'Thanks for the idea,' I told her. 'But there is no way Ryan and Leon are going to leave that place. They'd guess what I was up to.'

'There is one thing that would get them out of the way,' she said slowly, as if still piecing it together in her mind.

'And what would that be?' I tried to look a little more interested.

'If only you had the painting, you could tell them you'd meet up with them for a trade-off. Tell them they get the painting as along as they let you go.'

'You're forgetting just one important matter. I don't have the painting.'

'You could fake it.'

'Fake it?'

She got off my lap and sat next to me, leaning forward, eyes wide with excitement.

'Yes, fake it. It's easy. You have a photograph of the painting, remember? You showed it to me. All you have to do is to have it copied, enlarged, and framed!'

I hadn't the heart to tell her that this was the kind of scheme that a bright five–year-old would dream up. I let her play it out, hoping she'd hit all the obstacles I knew were there.

'What then?'

'Then you take a photo of the picture alongside that day's newspaper, to prove you've really got it. You must have seen them do that in the movies,' she added in exasperation. 'Then you send them the photo and suggest a meeting, somewhere a long way from their house. They want the painting badly, so they'll go.'

I waited at least ten seconds to tell her exactly what I thought of the idea.

'It's brilliant,' I said. 'Just brilliant.'

Now why hadn't I thought of it?

It was all set up. Next morning Nikki and Estelle went into town, where a photographer friend of Estelle's had a studio on Ocean Drive. On the telephone the previous night, he'd agreed to do us an enlargement of the photo to approximately the size of the painting, about twenty-four inches by eighteen. He was also going to mount it in an antique-style gilt frame. Of course, close-up, it wouldn't stand much scrutiny, but at distance on a photograph it might just be passable.

While they were gone, I wrote a note to Ryan saying that I had the painting here in California and the family had authorised me to act on their behalf. I said I hadn't disclosed that when we met at his house because I was checking him out, trying to assess how much he might pay for the painting. However, events had moved on, we were now long past negotiating and neither I nor the family wanted any more trouble. I was prepared to hand over the painting, and take the first plane back to the UK. I enclosed the photograph as proof. And I added that in view all that had happened I was uneasy about re-visting his house. I wanted the handover at a neutral location of my choosing.

It was a very thin story but there was just a chance that Ryan was so desperate for the painting, he would take the risk. If it turned out I was lying, he could still revert to his previous methods of getting what he wanted. He had nothing to lose. I suggested that if he would he meet me out on the coast road at One Tree Bay – a suitably lonely spot suggested by Nikki - the next evening at 6pm, I would hand over the painting. The deal would be that I gave him the picture, and he let me go back to the UK.

The plan was to send the letter together with the photo up to Ryan's house by courier. I had included my cellphone number in the note, and asked Ryan to ring to confirm the meeting. The letter which told him everything he needed to know. Except, of course, for just one thing. I didn't intend to be at the rendezvous.

10

The ocean was creeping onto the beach with weary lethargy. It was just before 8am. There was cool wind dancing around and high over the water, a gull banked and glided effortlessly, its black head and black wingtips stark against the icy blue of the sky. I was walking along the beach, the only sound the lazy tireless trudge of the sea. I had left Nikki sleeping, sneaking out so that I could have the serenity of the new day to get my mind set up. In an hour, the photograph and the letter would be couriered up to the villa and then all I had to do was wait to see if Ryan would take the bait. The more I thought about it, the more doubtful I became. Diversion schemes always work out in the movies because the script says so. Problem was, nobody was writing my script.

Trying to be more positive, I reminded myself that the photograph of the painting had worked out well. It had deliberately been taken medium-distance rather than close-up, so it could be seen and identified, but not studied in detail. I was kneeling alongside the painting holding a copy of yesterday's LA Times, the main headline easily visible.

My best estimate was that it was about fifteen miles between Ryan's house and the meeting point, on a twisting coastal road deserted for much of its length. Straggling tourists would be back in their hotels and apartments long before the appointed time of the meeting that would never take place. Nikki said the road followed the coastline, sometimes only a few metres from the waves, and I estimated that even a fast driver would need at least forty minutes to complete the round trip. Give Ryan and Leon a fifteen minute wait to work out I wasn't turning up and that gave me close on an hour at the villa, which should be enough. I knew from what Mahita had told me just where Ryan's gallery room was, and I intended to be pretty brutal with the door. If there was any evidence to link

Ryan to Marjorie and Krista, it would be in that room. It was a smooth, simple, minimal-risk plan that would work perfectly on screen for an action-hero like Matt Damon. Even Philip Marlowe would have somehow made it work. I was neither of them.

After an hour spent walking the beach I found myself near a boardwalk cafe, and I sat down for a coffee and croissant, The raw salty smell of the sea was in my nostrils, the old waiter had smiled at me, and for a few minutes at least, the world seemed a calm place where nothing nasty was going to happen. Early mornings gave me a curious detachment, provided a clarity of thought that I didn't get at other times. Maybe it was the absence of people, the the silence of the streets. Before too long, the day would wake. People would be out from their crumpled beds, locals on their way to mindless jobs, tourists looking for a cheap breakfast. For now, there were just a couple of joggers, bronzed limbs and slight frames, honing their fitness to a perfection I would never know. Their presence irritated me, marring my view of a flat glassy turquoise ocean meeting a clean virgin sky.

A couple of weeks ago I was six thousand miles away play-acting the easy life of the detective, sitting behind my big desk, when in walked Krista Carlton with her bright eyes and teasing top-button. And a DVD that made me sick when I saw a helpless old woman gunned down for a reason I still didn't know. I took the case because I'd seen too much of Bogart coming on to Lauren Bacall, read too much Philip Marlowe winning against the odds. And maybe because my ego needed a massage. Whatever the reason, I was stuck with it, a case where I knew the villain, knew the crime, but didn't know why it was committed and didn't have any evidence.

My theory was this: Ryan wanted the painting, reason unknown. Marjorie didn't want to part with it for sentimental reasons, and didn't need the money anyway. After his legitimate approaches by letter and lawyer had failed, Ryan decided to send an unmistakable message to the family. So he probably despatched Leon to kill Marjorie. The logic behind this horrific act was that Marjorie's next-of-kin would be likely to dispose of many of her possessions, including perhaps the painting. And if not, then they might be agreeable to selling it. But that didn't happen. The inheritance went to Krista, who also declined to sell because either she preferred the sentimental value of the picture to the money being offered, or more likely she just didn't make the connection between it and the murder of her aunt.

Next move, months later, is for Leon to again make a trip to the UK, this time to kill Krista. Then there could be no doubt the Carltons would get the message. Lose one member of your family to a hitman could perhaps be considered unlucky. But two? My initial supposition had been that it was a coincidence that Krista was murdered minutes after leaving my office but now it seemed more probable Leon had been following her and just took the opportunity when it presented itself. Otherwise, why not kill her before she came to see me?

It had to be Leon who had broken into my office - the distinctive shoes pointed to him as the intruder. I had to assume he found out Krista had seen a detective. It wouldn't have been difficult, I was part of headline news the day after the murder. Could be he then burgled my office in an attempt to discover just how much she had told me. So far, it was all assumptions and guesswork, but to me at least, it had at least some plausibility, made a sort of sense. I signalled the waiter, ordered more coffee and started to chew at my cold, rubbery croissant. The early sun had cleared the hills to the east and was gaining strength. I could feel its warming touch on my bare arms. At an adjacent table, a fat man with a paunch the size of a sofa stripped off his T-shirt.

I sipped a fresh coffee and continued to put the known facts and my fanciful theories into some semblance of order. Whether it was Leon or some hired help who tried to mow me down at the airport, I just didn't know. But it was as sure as it could be that Ryan and Leon were behind the hit-and-run attempt, and just as certain that they were responsible for mistakenly killing Lee instead of me. They didn't want me making enquiries into their activities. I was on the loose now only because when I visited their house, it suited them to let me go. Leon knew there would be a more convenient time and place. But I knew now that if I screwed up when I went back to the villa and got caught, then I didn't need to be a detective to work out the ending.

After almost two hours and four cups of coffee at the beach café, I walked slowly back to Estelle's. Putting it all in order had been worthwhile. My re-cap of the case made one thing absolutely clear. I still didn't really know what was going on.

It was about half an hour later, while I was in the shower, that my cellphone rang. Nikki brought it in to me, silently mouthing 'It's him' as I reached through the plastic curtain, still dripping. I grabbed at it frantically, squeezing water from my hair with my other hand.

'Hello Max.' I recognised the voice, that measured, deliberate, slightly smug voice. It was Leon. Don't you just hate it when a man who wants to kill you calls you by your first name?

'I have received an interesting item from you,' Leon said, as if he was merely confirming a pizza delivery. 'What you suggest would be a sensible conclusion.'

'That's good,' I said, trying to appear eager. 'You'll forgive my not wanting to come to your place. Last time I was there I did feel a bit threatened.'

'I understand perfectly,' said Leon. 'These things are best done on neutral territory.'

That would be hitman code for without witnesses. I confirmed the time and place and told him I just wanted to hand over the painting, go to the airport and leave.

'Best outcome for everyone,' said Leon mildly. 'See you later.'

11

It was a few minutes before 5pm and the heat was still solid and sultry. The air-conditioning in my car was set to maximum and the fan whined its protest as I headed north from Santa Monica on the Pacific Coast Highway. The sunlight was hazy, dulling the flat lifeless sea to thick molten glass. Over to my right, grand houses drifted by, homes built for movie stars in the 1930s but now also appearing washed out and less elegant in the strangely surreal light. The day seemed to be fading, and I started to feel uneasy. It was my intention to get to a vantage point near Ryan's house in time to ensure that both he and Leon left for our meeting. If there were any other staff left, I was going to have to take my chances. The domestic staff normally left at 4 pm, but maybe Ryan would be wily enough to leave someone, maybe the Antonio Banderas character, on guard.

As soon as I was in the vicinity, the first problem manifested itself. It became apparent that I couldn't get as close as I would need to be to witness the occupants of a vehicle leaving. I should have realised from my previous visits that Ryan's fortress was in an exposed location with virtually no cover nearby. If I got too close, my car would look suspicious - it might seem a little late in the day for a tourist to be in such a remote place. I just couldn't take the risk. Way past the house, at the first substantial curve, I swung the car off the road and managed to partially screen the Chrysler behind a clump of scrubby half-dead eucalyptus. My plan was to try to get nearer on foot, but right at the start, the plan began to go wrong. While I was creeping towards the house, dodging from rock to rock, I saw the big black Mercedes come fast out of the gates and sweep south at speed.

I was too still far away to see how many people were in the car. I just had to hope it was both of them. I was convinced

Leon would have to be there, if only to deal with me in his own murderous manner, and I was betting Ryan himself would want to be there as back-up, and also impatient to see the painting. They might even have taken a couple of guys with them as back-up, but I felt it was probably something they would rather handle on their own. They seemed a self-contained duo, unlikely to trust anyone else, and they wouldn't want witnesses. The car had left earlier than I had expected and maybe that indicated that they too were trying to get an advantage, perhaps planning to set something up at the meeting location. Not being able to see who was in the Mercedes was a major drawback, and I said a couple of short blunt words to myself. Once again I was off to an ominous start, having no idea of what I was up against so having to take chances.

Right now, with my hands sweating and my mouth dry, Nikki's brilliant idea didn't seem quite so brilliant. Right now, only a fool would go ahead. The fool took a pace forward, then started running, keeping low as if a sniper was on watch. In less than a minute, I was pressed hard against the outer wall in much the same place as I'd been the first time I'd got in. The dipping sun had broken through, coating the landscape in a thick rich amber and giving solid intensity to my shadow on the white wall. I stacked a few boulders against the wall to give me the increased height I required to get my hands over the top and then I scrabbled with my knees and toes until I could see over. This time I was screened by some tall shrubs which cleared the top of the wall so I pulled myself over and dropped down behind the foliage and lay there for a minute or two just watching. There was no sign of anyone around, and no sign of the Doberman, though that didn't mean he wasn't patrolling somewhere. Ryan's gallery was on the first floor, and the way up to that level was over the flat roof of the kitchen extension, as it was first time around. I crossed the open space slowly, not wanting my steps to make any sound that might alert the dog. Even so, every step seemed to detonate a magnified crunch that in the heightened tension sounded as if it would be heard at least a mile away. When I reached the kitchen wall, I flattened myself against it for a moment, then felt stupid doing so. If I hadn't been spotted by now, then I hadn't been spotted at all. Easing up to the window, I peeked inside. The room was empty.

I pulled myself up onto the roof, rolling flat and lying still, listening intently for any sound, however slight, which might suggest someone had seen me. Long stretched-out seconds passed but, from the outside at least, the place appeared deserted. It was so quiet you could have heard a silent prayer. French windows opened onto a railed rooftop patio area, but I could see they were shut. To the left, near where I had first seen the computer room, I noticed a window partly open. I crawled over like a trainee commando, scuffing my knees and elbows. Raising my head to the level of the sill, I could see into a bedroom. Pulling the window open, I climbed noiselessly in. It was a woman's bedroom, painted pale lemon. There was a French-style dressing table with gilt handles, a cream finish, and a large oval mirror. It's flat surface was crowded with cosmetics and a hair dryer. In the partly-open top drawer there was a selection of microscopic underwear. There was a massive double bed with white satin sheets and a cream cover. Three giant circular cushions were arranged neatly against the pillows. The bed was neatly made, fresh and crisp and there were no clothes draped around, no obvious signs of recent use apart from the junk on the dressing table, which presumably belonged to Ryan's new girlfriend.

Opening the door a few inches, I sneaked a look both ways down the corridor and saw nothing. For another half-minute I listened intently but all I heard was my own uneven breathing. According to Mahita's directions, I now needed to turn right because Ryan's gallery room was in that direction, just off the central landing. It would just take a few more cautious strides around the corner, and I should be on that landing, just feet from my target. I took one deep breath, one big step, and veered right. I should have looked round the corner first.

As I turned, I saw a man sitting in a chair opposite, apparently waiting for me. He was a man I hadn't seen before and he spoke to me in a voice I hadn't heard before.

'Good evening, Slater,' he said quietly. There was a slight

dusting of self-satisfaction to the tone. 'You are so predictable.'

I was looking at his face, trying to make an instant assessment, but something else caught my attention, a small movement of his hand at waist height. I glanced down and saw the ugly muzzle of Glock 22 gun.

12

It's not often I think about death, but when I do I always conclude there isn't a problem with death itself. The issue with death is the way it clings to the living. You're dead, you're gone, but your death clings to those left behind, making them sad, even distraught. That's what I don't like about death, the fact that it hurts those you love. Otherwise, you can take it, as long as it is reasonably quick.

When someone points a gun at you, it can focus your thinking. Bizarrely, I was thinking in just micro-seconds how Nikki was going to feel when my body was pulled out of the sea or maybe dug up from some shallow grave. I hoped she would wear a very short black dress at my funeral. I'd want to see some great legs before I left. And maybe she should wear a big wide-brimmed black hat and dark glasses and look as if she was a movie star attending the Cannes Film Festival and not my funeral. Image is important, even in death.

This strange visualisation of my own funeral was interrupted when Ryan stood up. He motioned with the gun that I should back away and then nodded at a pair of double doors just behind me. I went through and he followed. It was a large spacious study, with floor-to-ceiling bookcases, a big centrally-placed mahogany desk, and a scattering of brown leather chairs. It looked like the private library of a gentleman's' club. He told me – ordered me is more accurate - to sit down in the furthest armchair and added with chilling soft-spoken assurance that if I got out of the chair, he'd shoot me.

He stood in front of the desk, facing me and leaning against its edge, the gun pointing at my chest with resolute steadiness. I didn't know much about guns, but I'd seen enough American action movies to identify the Glock - common issue to the Stateside cops. I was a little disappointed that it wasn't the

357 Magnum favoured by Clint Eastwood's Dirty Harry character. If you're going to be shot dead, it might as well be with a cult gun.

Ryan was about fifty, maybe a little older, with strange wiry white hair that seemed to have given up trying to look like hair years ago. It seemed metallic, industrial, factory made. His face was pale and round and running to fat under the jaw and he had the bulging brown eyes of a bulldog, eyes that outwardly shone yet still somehow had a sterile deadness. He also had a scar on his cheek. The stitches were out but it was still savagely red, a big livid C-shape that mirrored the imprint of a wine glass rim. It was just below his left eye. I suddenly warmed to Mahita. She might be a fast-fading whore with an attitude as hard as a lump-hammer, but she had spirit. To glass Ryan even in the heat of an argument took courage. The only reason she was still alive was probably because Ryan felt she wasn't worth the effort. Women like her were just for using and discarding. They didn't talk afterwards because they knew that would merit violent retribution.

Ryan reached for a cellphone on the desk, locating it by touch, never looking away from me. The gun stared at me too with its lone mesmeric eye. His shirt was expensively cut but the effect was spoiled by poor colour choice, a dull pea green. It was open necked but with long sleeves, fastened by gold cufflinks with an onyx centre stone. His black trousers were razor-creased. His waist bulged a little over his wide leather belt and his stomach pushed at the shirt buttons as if it was trying to distance itself from him. He looked exactly what he was. A rich fat evil man.

He spoke quietly into the phone, flatly and mechanically. 'You can come back now, Leon,' he said. 'It was just as we thought.'

There was a pause while Leon made some comment and then Ryan said 'I have a gun on him but get back as soon as you can.'

Even when you're not a hero, you start to think of being a

hero, particularly when you know that your death is perhaps only minutes away. There was at least three metres of deep thick carpet between us and I'd no doubt even an Olympic sprinter would have been dead halfway across that expanse, let alone me. I put aside any thought of trying to lunge at him.

'So you're Slater,' he said thoughtfully. 'I was expecting someone... well, rather different.'

'I am different,' I said. 'You just don't know in which way.'

He continued to stare at me curiously. He appeared calm and controlled. His gun hand was steady, his manner relaxed. I'm good at reading people and I came to a firm conclusion almost immediately. I decided he would shoot me without hesitation.

It was a surprisingly soothing thought. When you're not sure of your fate, it can be worrying, stressful, skew your thinking and encourage you to take a risk. I'd never had a gun pointed at me before, and initially my instinct was to take any opportunity, however slim, to overpower Ryan. My mind had been racing, working on a trust-to-luck plan, the sort that always worked in Hollywood movies. Yet once I had decided such bravado was hopeless I became curiously relaxed, and with that came a determination to at least give Ryan some verbal aggravation. No point now in being quiet and subservient. It was time to needle him whenever possible, insult him, berate him, belittle him. Of course, as a survival plan it was useless, even childish. But as an immensely satisfying thing to do just before you die, it was flawless.

Ryan's glacial eyes stared at me, hard and unblinking. 'I know a great deal about you,' he said. 'I've done my research. I knew all about you before you ever left the UK, right from the time you were hired by the late Miss Carlton.'

'Late, thanks to you.'

'Do you watch many films, Slater?' Ryan asked. There was a note of amusement in his tone, as if he was sharing a private joke with himself.

'I like the movies,' I said cautiously, wondering where this was leading.

'Then in many films you will have seen that when the hero – that's you – confronts the villain - me - the villain gets an overwhelming urge to tell all, safe in the knowledge that the hero is about to die and that the confession would therefore be no use to him.'

I nodded.

'When I was a young man learning my business, I was always determined that I would never make such a confession,' he said. 'It seemed so stupid. In films, the hero always manages an amazing against-the-odds escape, alerts the police, and the villain gets caught.'

'Don't bet against it yet,' I said, but he ignored me.

'I have always thought that script writers and film directors were foolish to use such endings, because they would be contrary to real life experience.' He shifted position against the desk, moving back slightly so that he could actually sit on the edge. His feet dangled a couple of inches from the floor. The conversation hadn't affected his concentration. The gun was still pointing at me.

'However, I now find that I owe the film people an apology,' he said. 'I find that when you are actually in such a situation, there is a compelling urge to tell, to let someone know how brilliant you are. Do you not think that of all the fields of human endeavour, crime is the most undervalued?'

'I can do without your philosophical take on the world,' I said. 'Why don't you just tell me why you killed a helpless old woman in a wheelchair, and then her niece?'

Ryan was smiling now. It was the thin, under-nourished smile of someone who seldom practices the art. He shook his head, the big moon-shape rolling as if might topple loose. 'Wrong again, Slater. Leon takes care of that sort of thing for me. He's a professional who enjoys such work.'

'He's a cold sadistic bastard.'

'I'll pass on that description when he gets here,' said Ryan. 'I'm sure it will help his motivation. He'll be back in a few minutes, so you may as well enjoy a good story while you wait.' There was a certain eagerness in his voice, a desire to tell. I shrugged. I didn't have other plans.

'Do you know much about genealogy?'

'You mean beyond the fact that it's a tedious pastime?' I said.

He blinked twice. 'I wouldn't expect someone like you to understand,' he said.

'Someone like me?'

'Anyone with measurable intellect wouldn't be a private detective.'

'Hey, come on! I'll be getting upset in a minute.'

'Shut up,' he said sharply. 'This should interest you. It will fill in the blanks.'

'What makes you think there are any blanks?'

'If there weren't any blanks, you wouldn't be here. You'd be talking to the police.'

'OK. I made the connection between the Carlton killings and your interest in the painting, but then my luck ran out. Why kill for a painting that's worthless? Doesn't make sense.'

'To you, perhaps not.' The big man shifted his position on the desk, transferring his weight from left to right hip.

I watched the gun more than him. It was still in his hand, resting on his right thigh and still pointing in my direction.

'Family history interests me,' he began. 'It's a consuming interest, and once you delve into it, it becomes an obsession, a rewarding obsession. Over the past few years I have traced the Ryan family back to 1203.'

'Then you've probably found you're related to some murderous thieving scum,' I said. It wasn't a greatly witty comment but I was still trying to needle him.

Again, he ignored me. 'The Ryans started in Ireland, near Tralee, and worked on the land until the eighteenth century when one of them, Michael Ryan, married into a wealthy family.'

'Well, at least it beats fraud,' I said. 'I know all about your invoicing scam.'

'Fraud is itself an art form.'

'Talking of art, tell me about the painting,' I said. 'I'm getting bored.'

He was a hard man to rile. The corners of his mouth twitched upwards in the faintest of smiles, and he gently shook his head in mild admonishment. Nothing was going to get to him. He was enjoying his moment. I watched him carefully, his bulk perched on the edge of the desk, looking larger than he actually was because I was seated lower. He was again shifting position, settling back and getting comfortable. Here was a man who really wanted to tell his story. There was barely-suppressed excitement in his demeanour. The large head with the metallic hair was held high, the shoulders back. And while his gun hand was still steady, the fingers of his left hand were lightly drumming on the desk-top. This man wanted an audience, even if it was an audience of one. I suppose if you live in isolation and you have all the personal warmth of a polar wind, then it must be good once in a while to tell someone how great you are.

'Throughout the eighteenth and nineteenth centuries, my family prospered, became great land owners in Ireland,' he began. 'Then the fortune slipped away through a series of bad marriages and gambling. My grandfather Patrick came to England at the start of the first world war. Finding an old photograph of him in uniform was what started off my research. The need to keep finding out more becomes surprisingly compulsive. I have now compiled a detailed family history stretching back more than 800 years.'

'Just get to the part about he painting.'

'Ah yes. The painting is of my great-great-grandparents. It was painted in 1846. It is the only known image of them – it was before photography was invented. There were some family records of it being painted, and it has taken me four years to trace it. The last known record of it was when it passed out of the family and was sold at auction in 1932. I have a copy of the catalogue containing an illustration of it.'

'And eventually you traced it to the Carlton family?'

'Exactly. I had to acquire it, of course. It was rightly mine. Yet they wouldn't sell it, despite generous offers.'

I started laughing. I just couldn't help it. 'Come on, Ryan! You may not think I'm much of a detective, but even a less-than-bright kid wouldn't buy this! You're going to kill me away, so why not tell me the real story instead of this shit?'

A brief stab of pain seemed to cloud the bull-dog eyes.

'Come on, do it! Tell me the truth!' I said, my voice raised. 'Surely you don't expect me to believe you had a blind old lady in a wheelchair murdered just because she wouldn't sell you a picture of your ancestors! It's a fucking joke.'

Ryan leapt from the desk. He was fast for a fat man, swift and light and moving on the balls of his feet, and so rapidly he took me totally by surprise. Before I could even raise my arm, he whipped the gun in a short arc, the barrel slicing into my right cheek. This was the moment when Philip Marlowe would have snatched the gun, kneed the big man in the balls and sent him thudding into the thick carpet. But I wasn't Marlowe. I just sat there, stunned by the speed. I could feel the warm trickle of blood on my neck and a cold shiver of inadequacy everywhere else.

Ryan had quickly stepped back, and was now out of range again, breathing heavily but still completely in control of the situation. He stood there, red-faced, anger rippling through him. The right hand was at waist-height, the gun pointing at my chest.

'Do you still think it's a joke?' This time the voice actually had discernable emotion. 'I don't see you laughing now.'

'But you can't have people killed just for a painting.' I now believed he had, but I was playing up the incredulity, trying to buy some time.

'It was necessary,' said Ryan. He used the word necessary as casually as if the context was something as routine as breathing rather than as brutal as murder. 'I expected when the old woman was dead that the painting would come onto the open market, be auctioned. It clearly had sentimental value to her, but not to other members of the family. But it didn't happen.'

'And Krista Carlson? Necessary too?'

'She inherited the painting. I tried to buy it from her but she too refused.' He shrugged casually. 'Obviously, she had to be moved aside.'

'Obviously? Just how many people would you have moved aside as you put it, to get what you wanted? I suppose you would have wiped out the entire family?'

'It wouldn't have come to that. Somebody would have sold it, sooner rather than later. They would have got the message.'

'I can see genealogy hasn't taught you much respect for other peoples families.'

'All families get broken up one way or another,' said Ryan. 'It's part of history, an inevitable consequence of human nature. In any case, your touching indignation is misplaced. You seem to forget the painting is rightfully mine. My family commissioned it.'

'But generations later, they sold it. You lost ownership. You have to buy it back, not kill for it!'

'You are missing the point, Slater.' He took a pace forward as if ensuring I wouldn't miss a word. 'Let me tell you something about myself. I was born in Liverpool, into a poor family. My father was unemployed, and a drunk. My mother ran away with a man who treated her only marginally better. Even as a child I was intelligent enough to realise my only way out was education. I put myself though college, then studied accountancy. I was determined to become rich. I achieved that ambition.'

'I suppose fraud was a good career move,' I said. I didn't much care now. The alien manner in which he had cast aside the killing of Marjorie and Krista, regarding them as just insignificant obstacles, was chilling. And I hadn't even mentioned Lee.

'Fraud was just a fast route to wealth. I could have done it by honest means had I wished. Let me tell you something about money, Slater. When you're poor, you imagine that if you become rich you will be able to buy anything you want. Mostly, you can, of course. But if you become rich, find there is something you must have but then discover that money can't buy it, do you know how angry that makes you feel?'

'What's the weather like?' I asked suddenly.

'What?'

'The weather. What's it like?'

Ryan glanced over to the window. The orange orb of the sun was low on the skyline.

'As you can see, the weather is fine,' he snapped, fazed by the shift of subject.

'Not here,' I said. 'I meant on your planet. You know, Planet Psychopath.'

That got the result I wanted. Ryan stepped forward and lashed out with the gun. This time my forearm took the force of the blow, deflecting it so it just clipped the top my head. But there was not going to be a movie-style wrestle for the gun. He'd seen the movies too. Again he stepped smartly out of range and my chance had gone. This time he raised the gun, pointing it directly at my chest. He was less than ten feet from me, too far away for me to leap and too close for him to miss. Every shred of my concentration became focussed on Ryan's right hand. My vision had become telescopic. I saw the skin of his forefinger whiten as it started to put pressure on the trigger.

13

I was half a second from seeing Nikki in that short black dress, wide-brimmed hat and movie-star dark glasses, standing distraught at my funeral. Then there was the loud crunch of car wheels on the gravel driveway, and a flash of relief on Ryan's face as he strode over to the window to glance out. If the distraction hadn't come at that moment, I believed he would have killed me. He was right on the edge.

As he walked over to the window, Ryan was still careful, always watching me, the gun still pointing my way. He glanced down to the driveway and then back to me. 'Leon is here,' he said. 'I'm sure he can persuade you to tell us where the painting is.'

'Did you forget the painting? A minute ago you were all set to shoot me. But if I do tell you, do we still have a deal?' Unlikely, but it was worth a try.

'I admire your optimism. There was never going to be a deal. And I would have shot you in the stomach. Takes a while to die, long enough for you to talk'.

I'd already guessed that. And I knew that as soon as Leon came into the room, I'd be in for a brutal beating, probably some torture, and eventually I'd be killed and buried in remote scrubland or dumped in the sea.

The sound of the front door being opened carried up the huge open staircase followed by rapid footfall on the wooden stairs. My chair was about six feet from the French windows, old Colonial style with lots of small panes. As Ryan made a half-turn as Leon came into the room, I leapt from the chair and flung myself at the double doors, slamming them hard with my left shoulder at the central and weakest point. There was a rending of wood as the bolts ripped free and I burst through, falling to the ground and rolling onto the balcony. There was shouting behind me and a gunshot cracked, but I was already over the balcony rail and dropping ten feet to the ground. I raced to the front of the house to get to Leon's Mercedes, the pump of adrenalin fuelling just one brain-burning thought. There was no need for Leon to have taken the key out of the ignition.

He'd pulled up outside his own house. He was in a rush to get inside. He would have left the key in the ignition. God, let it be there!

It was.

I started the car, slammed the automatic shift into drive and floored the pedal, taking a sharp clockwise arc, machine-gunning gravel from the rear wheels. The light was fading fast now but in the rear view mirror I could see two figures running towards a Ford Taurus I'd seen parked at the side of the house. By the time I had reached the open gateway, it was already starting after me.

There was a squeal of tyres from the Mercedes as they bit into the tarmac and I headed south down the coast road, the same route Leon had taken. I was driving fast but already the Taurus was right up behind me and I could see it was Leon at the wheel. My only chance was to keep going until I got to the outskirts of Santa Monica maybe six or eight miles further on. But seconds later on the first straight stretch of tarmac, despite my straddling the centre of the road, the Taurus began to swing out, the prelude to an attempt to come alongside. Just as it did so, I hit the brake pedal as hard as I could, hoping the action would force the Taurus to swerve violently to avoid smashing into the back of the Mercedes.

It did swerve out, slipping past me as I decelerated and when it tried to cut back in I wrenched the steering wheel hard to the right, hitting the rear corner of the Taurus and at the same time I floored the accelerator for a surge of mighty V6 power. The heavy Mercedes, two tons of prime German metal, rammed the Taurus, barely half its weight, slewing it off the road and across the verge. I watched transfixed as it careered ahead of me, losing momentum as it ploughed across the narrow strip of dusty earth towards the cliff top. It slammed into a ridge of large boulders and flipped over, a graceful rotating somersault which ended with exploding glass and rending metal as it smacked onto its roof and slid screeching and scraping over loose rocks. I expected it to plunge over the edge, but it didn't. In an extraordinary freak of fate the Taurus came to rest on the very edge of the drop, still on its roof, hanging there as if undecided. It's front half jutted like a big chin, a stark silhouette thrusting out towards the blood-red sunset sky.

I clambered recklessly over the rocks to get to it. The car lay like a huge dying animal, beaten and broken, its strangled last breath hissing from a smashed radiator. Kneeling down at the side of it, I looked in through the gaping glassless windows. The airbags were limp. They had cushioned the initial impact but were then impotent for the subsequent crash landing after the somersault. Leon was dead. He hadn't been wearing his seat belt and his neck broken, head at ninety degrees, his face a messy mask speared with shards.

Ryan was still alive. He was belted in and he hung upside down, head resting against the caved-in roof. He was bleeding a little from his mouth and I guessed he probably had internal injuries, but his eyes were open and alert. When he saw me peering at him he reached out, hand trembling like that of a feeble beggar.

Given the severity of the crash, I was surprised he had survived and though I found it hard to admit, I was also disappointed he was still alive. His death would have been a neat, convenient end to the whole nightmare caper, a final black line under it. A walk-away-with-a clear-conscience black line. His death would have obviated the need for any further action. There would be no more probing, no more guessing, no more tough decisions.

Ryan was guilty – he'd confessed eagerly and with pride – but that confession apart, I had no proof at all of his involvement in at least two murders. Cheating a deserved death even by chance meant that Ryan was still a problem, still a cunning, dangerous adversary who even at this moment might still hold an ace card. I could see it all unfolding. I summon help. The paramedics arrive. Ryan appears badly hurt but injuries can look worse than they are. They get him to hospital and find all he has are two broken ribs and a cut lip. Even while the X-rays are being checked, he's on the phone to his lawyer. Then his smart lawyer talks to the cops. The lawyer explains how a deranged Englishman with a bizarre story about an old painting breaks into Ryan's house and threatens him. Mr Ryan and his friend Leon, both respected businessmen and California residents, have to flee their property in fear of their lives. The crazy Englishman chases them in one of their own cars, forcing them off the road and killing nice inoffensive Mr Leon. The damaged Mercedes is a silent witness for the prosecution, backing up the staff who will testify to seeing me barge in to Ryan's house on a previous occasion. The likely outcome would be Max Slater, the inept detective, spending the next 20 years in San Quentin developing a taste for cockroach-flavoured food.

For a minute or two, I pondered this grim prospect, but then began to tell myself I was just getting panicky, blowing it all out of proportion. I'd have my own lawyer, some intervention from the British Embassy, and Boyd and Nikki to back me up. There would be enquiries, evidence would be uncovered. Maybe.

I wasn't sure. I wasn't sure about anything. If someone had asked my shoe-size right then, I'd have to guess. Ryan was still staring at me, his eyes animated and despite his predicament, still glaringly with hate. Suspended upside-down, trapped by his own weight on the seat-belt, he hung like an obese giant bat, his face swollen red with the down-flow of blood.

What the hell was I going to do? The easy way out was simple, and very, very tempting. If I dragged him out of the car and smashed a boulder onto his head, it would solve everything. It would just look as if he had been thrown clear of the car when it overturned. Question was, could I do it? Killing another human being, however despicable a creature they might be, was in my view fundamentally against human nature. It's one thing believing you could turn killer if your own life was threatened. Maybe some could. But my life wasn't being threatened. Right now, Ryan was helpless and it would take the kind of nerve I didn't have to just coldly and clinically kill him. That decision meant I had to get help for Ryan. There was a hospital in Santa Monica. An ambulance could get here in about 15 minutes. I had to make the call. I dug into my pocket for my cellphone.

The sun, still large and colour of a tangerine, hung just above the waterline and the sea lay quiet and untroubled, a dappled golden sheet with scalloped flecks of crimson gently shuffling and shifting. Behind me, the dusty landscape was darkening. Inching forward, I looked over the edge of the cliff. There was a drop of about thirty metres onto big rocks, waves slapping at them without effort. They seemed to be slowing as I stared at them. Everything was slowing, coming to a stop. Into this mystical tranquillity came a snapshot of Marjorie. It materialised above the sea, small black and white pieces drifting in from all directions and then fusing together to form a spectral image of a crippled old lady, head slumped as if in sleep but with that third baleful eye in her forehead. I'd always felt angry about the manner in which Marjorie had died, a cold corrosive anger I felt would never leave me. Now came the sadness, a sweeping bitter sadness that swelled salt-tears in my eyes. I blinked repeatedly, the tears sliding away one by one. Then the picture of Marjorie began to fade, disintegrating like sepia sand and trickling into the sea.

It was replaced by a vivid, shocking close-up of Krista Carlton's face, eyes wide and scarlet lips slightly parted as she lay back in the seat of her BMW with blood still seeping from the holes in her head. I couldn't look away. My eyelids were jammed open, my head locked in position. For what seemed like many minutes, I was forced to watch the death-face of Krista Carlton, pallid and punishing, yet still intensely beautiful. Eventually, that image faded too and I was left trembling.

Marjorie and Krista were telling me Ryan should die. Their voices were strong and howled and echoed from their long dark corridors directly into my soul. But I just couldn't do it. They were asking too much of me. I didn't have the courage, and I didn't have the right. My old Sunday School teacher was strong on the Ten Commandments. Thou shalt not kill.

The phone was still gripped in my left hand and I knew I had to call 911. I lifted the Samsung but the screen was blank. I pressed the on button but nothing happened. The battery was dead.

I took that as a message straight from God.

I now knew with unshakable certainty why I had been brought to this desolate cliff top with its fiery sky and disturbing bleached-out visions. How long had I been there? I didn't know. I'd lost all sense of time and somehow couldn't focus on my watch. Time had stilled, missed a beat, halted on its eternal journey. It was a long sunset.

By now, it should be dark, the first stars low in the heavens, bright against the deep plush of flawless indigo blue. Yet inexplicably, the sun was still there, stuck on the horizon, a smouldering ball that refused to leave the scene. There was no need to think what to do. I found myself doing it. I picked up a boulder about the size of a football ball and with new strength, eased it onto the underside of the upturned Ford, shoving the boulder along, inching towards the section which hung over the edge. Then I picked up another and did the same again. This one rolled slightly and wedged by a suspension strut. Methodically, I pushed and lobbed more boulders towards the extremity of the giant metal see-saw, a dozen, maybe two dozen. Some were as large as I could lift, others merely the size of a grapefruit. I just kept heaping them on until slowly the Taurus began to tilt just one or two degrees with an eerie metallic groan.

Pausing in my task, I knelt down again and looked in at Ryan. His eyes were still open, bewildered brown glass marbles set in puffed-up dough. His mouth was trying to say something, the rubbery blood-stained lips gaping like a landed fish. Lying flat on my stomach alongside the car, I manoeuvred so that my face was on the same level as Ryan's. He was trying to say something, but couldn't speak. But I was sure he could still hear, so I extended my arm and pointed through the glassless windscreen, out to the horizon.

'Take a good look at the sunset,' I said, my voice hard. 'It's the last one you'll ever see. They don't have them in hell.'

The glass eyes reacted. They blinked just once. The lips moved too, but no sound came out.

Standing up, I brushed some debris from my shirt, and then set about doing what I had to do. I piled another boulder onto the front of the car. And another. By now, the crumpled bonnet was tilting steeply towards the sea, and the next boulder sent the car over. It dropped vertically, smashing nose-first against the rocks and then toppling onto its roof, creating a soft, muffled splash in the water.

I stood on the edge looking down. Wide horizontal bands of rich light from the long sunset highlighted the underside of the car, its exposed suspension arms and snaking exhaust system looking like grim alien entrails. The sea had lost some of its lethargy, almost imperceptibly it was picking up pace. Small hungry waves converged on the wreck, nipping at it like strange, unformed ravenous creatures. Dark water swirled in, quickly filling the car and it soon slid from sight. I didn't know if at this moment Ryan was dead from the impact or was drowning. I just stood in the long sunset with the lingering ghosts of Marjorie and Krista until finally, the great golden light went out.

When I turned away from the sea, the sky and the ghosts and walked over to the Mercedes, I was shaking. I had to lean against the car for a while until my emotions returned from their whirlwind ride. I kept breathing long and deep, filling my lungs, driving down the oxygen until my heart-rate slowed and I could look at my hands and see that the tremors had ceased.

The Mercedes had a dented front wing and a headlight was out, but it was still drivable. I got in, the cream leather cool through my shirt and causing me to suddenly shiver. My mind seemed to be operating in automatic mode, my thoughts too scattered to be quickly retrieved. Instinct had taken over, moving my limbs, driving the car. I found myself heading back up the deserted road towards Ryan's house. The place was quiet when I got there, no lights on, no other cars around, no sign of activity. Wherever the dog was, he wasn't barking. I guessed Ryan had given everyone the night off to make sure he and Leon were alone to deal with the situation. It would be the morning before any staff arrived, and even then it might be a few more hours before they realised their bosses were missing, rather than just out.

A pale quarter-moon was climbing in the east, casting thin diluted light across the building, silvering its white stucco frontage and blackening its deep shadows. I parked the Mercedes at the rear of the house, wiping everything I thought I might have touched, and then I went around to the front door, which was still open, and went in. There was no longer any no need to probe its shabby secrets, no need to locate the family gallery and gaze on the ranks of Ryan's ancestors. They could tell me nothing now. But there was one thing I had to do. While Ryan was telling me his life story, I'd seen the photograph of the painting and the note I had sent him lying on his desk. I retrieved them, and left.

I walked almost jauntily out of the gates and down the road to retrieve my Chrysler from where I had left it about a hundred years ago. I didn't know what the police were going to make of the situation when they eventually found the Taurus on the beach. Someone would see it when the tide went out, some early morning fisherman or keen jogger. Chances were it would be put down as an accident. The injuries would be consistent with the crash, a car being driven too fast and losing control. OK, there was a scraped wing on the Mercedes, but that was parked back at the house and the police may not connect it with the crash. The important thing was that there was no way I could be connected with it. There were only three of us involved, and the other two were dead. All I had to do now was work out something I could tell Nikki. Because I couldn't tell her what I'd done. It would be too tough for someone else to live with that kind of knowledge.

Nikki and Estelle were sitting at the kitchen table when I got back, sharing a bottle of white wine. It was a comforting domestic scene, so warmly reassuring and safe after the trauma and stress of the past few hours that I stood there looking at them, glad they were there just being so ordinary, so normal. Nikki jumped up and rushed towards me, her face taut with alarm. I had forgotten the gash to my cheek from Ryan's gun. The blood had long dried but the wound probably looked worse than it was. Her eyes widened with concern, and she was sobbing into my shoulder, hugging me close and trying to say all the comforting clichéd phrases I desperately wanted to hear.

Estelle left the room, silently mouthing 'good night' and closing the door quietly. Nikki looked up, eyes red and streaked with tears, but a little calmer now.

'What happened?' she asked. 'Did you get the evidence?'

'I got caught,' I said. 'But it doesn't matter anymore. Ryan and Leon chased after me but their car left the road south of Malibu and went over the cliff. I went back to check and I saw their car sink. They're both dead. It's all over now.'

I was being economic with the truth, but I just couldn't tell her how I'd helped Ryan on his way to hell. It would be hard enough for me to live with, let alone her. She was looking at me wide-eyed, her hand over her mouth. 'Have you called the police?'

'There was no need. It was just an accident. I thought it best not to get involved.'

Nikki reached up and placed her hands behind my neck, pulling me towards her.

'You're shaking,' she said.

' Tough day.'

She led me upstairs, one slow step at a time. Each step got higher. The final two seemed to be waist level. By the time we reached our room, I was leaning on her, dragging my legs, stumbling with exhaustion, drained by the emotional aftermath of a surreal act of personal justice. Easing myself onto the bed, I lay staring at the ceiling fan, its blades motionless and unthreatening. Nikki perched beside me, her cool fingertips touching my face as if she could heal. Leaning over, she kissed my forehead, just the lightest possible brush of her lips.

I slipped fast and unresistingly into a deep and sinless sleep.

ALSO BY NICK FLETCHER

IMPERFECT DAY

Private eye Max Slater is initially reluctant to take on a case which involves him having to decipher an enigmatic message from a man who died 15 years earlier, but the person asking for his help was the entrancingly beautiful Grace and he finds her plea irresistible. Soon, Slater finds himself taking on a psychotic millionaire who appears to murder by proxy and who sees Slater standing between him and a fortune in stolen diamonds.

Set mainly around Brighton on the south coast of England, this fast-action thriller sees Max Slater once again having to step outside the law in his quest for justice.

'Laced with barbed comments on modern life, piercing observation of human foibles and often near-poetic imagery, it's style is cool, distinctive and direct.'

ALSO BY NICK FLETCHER

SNAPSHOT

Snapshot is a collection of Max Slater novellas which find the flawed private detective caught up in six extraordinary and compelling cases, each requiring him to push his investigative skills – and sometimes his luck – to the limits.

They include an act of cold calculated vengeance in the sultry heat of a Spanish holiday resort, a famous thriller writer involved in a real-life murder in the idyllic French countryside and a pornographic photo the only clue to a shocking double killing in an English seaside town.

'As an anti-hero private eye frequently out of his depth, Max Slater commands the attention immediately as he walks the tightrope of moral dilemma in seeking truth and justice.'